"He's coming back this way!"

The man searching the river had reversed course and was now coming back toward them. The two men with lights were closing in on them.

"We need to get out of here."

Hollis grabbed Laura's hand and led her uphill. When she looked down, she could see the two lights and the bridge with the car parked by it. The car was abandoned. Could they get to that car before the men did?

A force burst out of the darkness and knocked Hollis over. Laura had been standing so close to him that she fell back on her behind. Soldier had found them.

He was on top of Hollis hitting him in the face.

Laura picked up a stick preparing to hit Soldier.

"Stay back." Soldier pulled a knife from his belt.

Laura stopped a few feet from him. Hollis wasn't moving. Had Soldier managed to knock him out?

Then, Soldier raised the knife, preparing to drive it into Hollis's chest.

Ever since she found the Nancy Drew books with the pink covers in her country school library, **Sharon Dunn** has loved mystery and suspense. Most of her books take place in Montana, where she lives with three nearly grown children and a hyper Border collie. She lost her beloved husband of twenty-seven years to cancer in 2014. When she isn't writing, she loves to hike surrounded by God's beauty.

Books by Sharon Dunn

Love Inspired Suspense

Montana Standoff
Top Secret Identity
Wilderness Target
Cold Case Justice
Mistaken Target
Fatal Vendetta
Big Sky Showdown
Hidden Away
In Too Deep
Wilderness Secrets
Mountain Captive
Undercover Threat
Alaskan Christmas Target
Undercover Mountain Pursuit
Crime Scene Cover-Up
Christmas Hostage

Visit the Author Profile page at LoveInspired.com for more titles.

CHRISTMAS HOSTAGE

SHARON DUNN

LOVE INSPIRED SUSPENSE
INSPIRATIONAL ROMANCE

LOVE INSPIRED® SUSPENSE

INSPIRATIONAL ROMANCE

ISBN-13: 978-1-335-58801-2

Recycling programs
for this product may
not exist in your area.

Christmas Hostage

For questions and comments about the quality of this book, please contact us
at CustomerService@Harlequin.com.

Love Inspired
22 Adelaide St. West, 41st Floor
Toronto, Ontario M5H 4E3, Canada
www.LoveInspired.com

Printed in U.S.A.

To every thing there is a season,
and a time to every purpose under heaven.
—*Ecclesiastes* 3:1

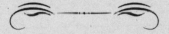

The book is dedicated to all my faithful readers.
Thank you for taking the often dangerous
and always romantic journey with my characters.

ONE

Even before the shouting and the woman's scream, Laura Devin sensed that something was wrong in the lobby of First Federal Bank. The three seconds of silence signaled danger to her. The bright morning conversation between bank employees stopped abruptly, but it was what she saw on her computer screen seconds after logging on that told her they were in the middle of a bank robbery. All the alarms and cameras had been disabled, just like with the other small-town banks that had been robbed in the last two years.

Her back was to the open door in the room next to the lobby, where she was working at a computer. When she whirled her chair around, she could only see the back of one of the tellers. Then she saw a flash of movement on the other side of the counter. One of the tellers screamed.

Then the shouting.

"This is a bank robbery. Do as I say, and no one will die here today."

Even if one of the tellers had time to push the silent alarm, it had been disabled. The police would not show up.

Laura's gaze jolted to her purse across the room, where her phone was. The door was open. If she went for it, they might see her. Closing the door even partway would alert the robbers to her presence that much faster. But she had no choice. She had to make that call.

She sprinted across the carpet and grabbed her phone, pressing 911.

"Hey, there's somebody in that room. Get her."

The operator came on the line. "What is your emergency?"

"Bank robbery—"

A hand went over her mouth. She dropped the phone before the thief could grab it from her. He must have seen that she was making a call, or at least heard the phone when it landed on the carpet. And yet, he didn't tell her to pick it up. Maybe it was still on and the operator could hear what was happening. Would the police be able to determine the location of the bank and get here in time?

He whispered in her ear, the fabric of the ski mask he wore brushing over her cheek. "It's going to be okay. Just do what they say."

His voice held a gentle, warm quality.

"Hurry up." The voice from the lobby was harsh and intense.

Once the first robber, the one with the soft voice, had pulled her into the lobby, she took in the scene. Three other men in ski masks, all with guns. The two female bank employees were huddled together by the Christmas tree.

The man with the harsh voice pointed the gun at Laura. "What is she doing here? There's only supposed to be two of you."

Laura's heart raced. If they found out she was a computer expert hired to beef up security in the bank because of the robberies, she'd be shot on the spot.

The teller whose name was Ruby spoke up. "New hire. Just started today."

The other teller, Angela, an older woman, added between sobs and gasps, "We've been really busy because of Christmas."

These two women, whom she'd only met this morning, had just saved her life.

The thief with the gentle voice still gripped her arm but didn't point his gun at her. Something was really off about this guy. Like he didn't want to be here doing what he was doing.

"Over there with the other two." The thief with the harsh voice seemed to be the one in charge. His build suggested that he was in his twenties or thirties, and in good shape.

One of the other thieves stood by the door while he aimed the gun toward the two women. It was clear from the steadiness of his stance that if they moved, he would shoot to kill.

The fourth thief paced the floor, clearly nervous. He was tall and lean. She couldn't even guess at his age.

Gentle Voice tugged her arm.

"Hurry up. Just push her over there with the others," said the thief in charge, waving his gun.

Gentle Voice pressed on her back. "You heard him. Get over there." He made his voice sound intense but not in a scary way.

The leader stomped toward the other two tellers. "Which one of you knows the code to the vault?"

Angela raised a trembling hand.

The leader lifted his chin and waved his gun in such a way to signal that she needed to move. He pointed the gun at Ruby. "You need to open all the teller drawers. Don't try anything or Joe here will shoot you." He indicated the tall nervous man.

Joe aimed his gun at Ruby as she stepped toward the counter.

Laura thought she heard sirens.

Angela took a step toward the vault. The

leader grabbed the older woman's arm and jerked her toward him.

The sirens grew more distinct. Her call had gone through. The police were on their way.

Joe turned his head toward the window, where approaching police cars could be seen. His voice filled with anguish. "Oh, no."

The leader pounded his fist on a counter. "How did this happen?"

Laura saw that the robbers had placed another gun by the door. The robber with the steady hands holstered his handgun and picked up what looked to be an automatic rifle.

The next minute went by in a turmoil-filled unfolding of violence and shouting.

"To the van," shouted the leader.

Joe, the nervous one, headed toward the teller counter. "We've got to have something to show for our effort." He jumped over the counter and grabbed some cash from a drawer that Ruby must have opened. He stuffed the money in his pocket.

"Move, now," the leader shouted.

The man with the automatic rifle was already headed toward the doors.

The police looked to be about a block away. The intensity of the sirens surrounded Laura as her heart pounded. She could see flashing lights through the lobby window.

The leader grabbed Laura and pressed the gun to her temple. "You're our life insurance policy."

"No hostages," said Gentle Voice.

"Shut up," said the leader. "Who's in charge here?"

The man with the rifle took the lead as they moved toward the door. He opened fire before the police cars could pull into the parking lot. Lights flashing, three police cars stopped. The officers got out, taking cover behind their vehicles. Shots were exchanged and one of the robbers cried out in pain.

An officer shouted, "They've got a hostage. Hold your fire."

Snapshots of the street, the police and the other bank robbers flashed past Laura as she was dragged across the parking lot. Cold winter wind whipped across her skin. The robber's tight grip on her arm pressed on a nerve, sending pain through to her shoulder and making her want to pull away.

The van doors were flung open, and she was tossed inside. Two of the other robbers jumped in the back with her before the doors slammed shut. Her stomach pressed against the cold metal of the van floor. And then, the van was rolling at a high speed while the gunfire resumed.

The van zigzagged through small-town streets

just coming alive with morning traffic and then down several alleyways. The man with the gentle voice and the one named Joe were in the back with her while the leader and Steady Hand sat up front.

"She's no longer useful to us. Let's ditch her," Gentle Voice said through gritted teeth as he pressed his hand against his shirt. She noticed it was stained with blood.

"You're hurt." Laura leaned toward him.

The answer to Gentle Voice's suggestion came from the leader after he checked the rear-view mirror and glanced out the side window. "We can't stop. Cops are still on our tail."

The van continued to careen wildly as Steady Hand drove at a high speed.

Laura leaned toward the injured man. "Did you get shot?" All she saw was his brown eyes.

"It's nothing." It was clear from the sharp, quick breaths he took that he was in pain.

Joe rocked back and forth and then pulled off his ski mask. "You said easy money. You said in and out."

Joe was probably barely out of his teens. He had acne scars and wild hair that stuck out at odd angles.

The leader turned slightly. "You took your mask off. Now she can identify you."

"What does it matter? This whole thing has gone south. The mask makes me sweat."

The leader turned back to face the windshield, talking under his breath. "I don't know why things went sideways like that. Gotta figure that out. Maybe we were set up."

Laura locked on to Gentle Voice's gaze.

He said nothing. He must have seen her make that call. Why was he protecting her?

The van increased speed. Though she could not see much, it was clear that they were on a country road. She wrapped her arms around her body. Even with the van heater on, she was cold without a winter coat.

Ten minutes passed. The road became rougher, jostling her and the other two men on the van floor.

She listened in terror to the conversation between the driver and the leader.

"We lost them. I think we can dump her now. It's a long walk back to town," said Steady Hand.

"She can identify Joe. Who knows what else she can tell the police. We have to get rid of her...permanently," said the leader.

Her breath caught and her heart pounded.

Gentle Voice groaned in pain. Almost involuntarily, she drew closer to him. "Are you okay?"

"This gunshot wound is worse than I thought. I need medical help." He pulled her close and whispered in her ear. "Lie to save your life."

It took her only a second to realize what he was suggesting. "I put myself through college as an EMT. I can take care of his wound."

The leader turned around in his seat. His eyes narrowed as he stared at her. "Do what you got to do to keep him alive."

"Might as well take this off." The driver pulled off his ski mask. Steady Hand had an abundance of dark hair and a neck tattoo. He rubbed his face. "That thing makes me itch."

"Good idea." The leader took his mask off as well, revealing his blond hair. "Once she's no longer useful we're going to have to do away with her, anyway."

Her heartbeat whooshed in her ears as she tried to fight off paralyzing numbness. Gentle Voice had bought her some time, but she knew she did not have long to live.

Applying pressure to his injured shoulder and pectoral muscle, undercover FBI Agent Hollis Pryce sucked in a breath and drew his shoulder blades together as pain shot through his body. Maybe he was hurt worse than he realized. His winter coat had been unzipped when the bullet grazed him. He could see the exit wound in the fabric of his upper sleeve. A round circle with down feathers sticking out.

The dark-haired woman rubbed the forearm

of his uninjured shoulder as if to offer comfort. His mind thought of a hundred things as the van wound its way deep into the Montana mountains.

After nearly a year of work to get close to the bank robbers, this was the first time he'd been invited to be a part of the heist. It wasn't these robbers Hollis was ultimately after. They would be easy enough to arrest and then other robbers would take their place. The only way to end the heists was to find out who was behind the robberies. Who was the man doing all the planning? It seemed the only way to do that was to go deep undercover, win the trust of the robbers and hopefully find out who was in direct communication with the mastermind.

The woman beside him must have had time to call the police. It had been an impossible choice. If he had outed her, she would have been shot right away. The police showing up had meant the heist would not go as planned. As with the other robberies, the intel for this one had been impeccable, which made Hollis think someone on the inside fed the crew information and planned the robberies. In the last two years, there had been eight of them in small towns across Montana, Wyoming and Idaho.

The dark-haired woman gazed at him. "I can take your mask off if you like. Everyone else has."

"I can get it." He took his good hand off the shoulder wound only to feel a new level of pain. He clamped it back in place. How much blood had he lost? He'd been a medic in the army before joining the Bureau. He assumed the bullet had passed through muscle and not hit a vital organ. He'd be in much worse shape if it had. The wound needed to be treated, but right now he just wanted to apply pressure to stop the bleeding. He leaned his head forward. "Maybe you should take it off."

She pulled off the knitted ski mask.

He thought he saw trust in her eyes. How had this gone so wrong as to involve a civilian? He had only delayed her death. In the brief time he'd gotten to know these men, he knew that the man in the driver's seat, the one who called himself Soldier, would not bat an eyelash at killing someone.

None of the men used their real names. Part of the genius planning of the robberies. If any of them were caught, they wouldn't be able to give much information to the police about the others.

He and Joe were the new recruits. It had taken a year of gaining the trust of the criminal underworld in Wade County before he finally hit pay dirt and got connected with the man who vetted potential thieves for the robberies, the man sitting in the passenger seat who called himself Branson. Other agents had been planted in other rural areas with no results. To these men, he was Derrick, a petty thief who had hitched west from Chicago. Just another criminal looking for a big score.

Though the crew was never the same four guys, Soldier and Branson had given away that they had participated in at least half the robberies.

Joe continued to run his hands through his hair and rock back and forth, while the woman remained close to Hollis, a look of concern etched across her face.

What a mess this had become. There had to be a way to help this woman escape and not blow his cover. But right now, trying to manage the pain made it hard to think.

The van came to a stop. They were at their hideout.

"We need to talk." Branson addressed his comment to Soldier, and he turned to the back. "Joe, help the woman get Derrick inside." He lowered his voice half an octave. "Make sure she doesn't get any ideas."

Joe slid open the side door and jumped out. Sweat dripped into Hollis's eyes. He could discern the evergreens and the first building of the abandoned resort that the thieves had established as their hideout a day before. They were miles from civilization. Cell phones didn't work up here, but there was little chance of the police finding them in such a forgotten place.

The woman got out as well and then leaned back inside to address Hollis. "Can you scoot to the edge here and then maybe he can get under your good arm?" She nodded toward Joe.

"No way," said Joe, pulling his gun from his waistband and pointing it at the woman. "I got my orders. You'll just try something. You carry him."

"Let me get over there first," said Hollis.

He pressed his lips together to keep from groaning, while with some effort, he scooted toward her. He noticed her glancing all around, maybe assessing the possibility of escape, or just taking in the unexpected surroundings. The resort had been huge in its time but was now overgrown and crumbling.

The dilapidated sight of what had once been a main meeting house surrounded by smaller cabins was probably a surprise. There was a concrete building with half the roof missing that had once housed showers.

From somewhere in the camp Hollis could hear the raised voices of Branson and Soldier. He ignored them as he lifted his good arm so the woman could get under him for support. He tried not to lean too heavily on her as they walked, with Joe following off to the side, still holding the gun.

Hollis indicated the larger building. His cot and belongings were by a crumbling fireplace. Parts of the ceiling had caved in, leaving gaping holes where light shone in. Fallen beams slanted across the floor and everything was covered with debris. He'd chosen to set up camp in the part of the building that looked the most stable by the fireplace. Building a fire helped keep the area warmer.

The woman helped him sit down on the cot while Joe kept an eye on her. His bed had never felt so good. Even the slightest movement caused him pain.

"You'll probably want to lie down," said the woman. "Let me lift your legs and you can lie back."

Once his feet were stretched out on the bed, she removed his boots, placed his sleeping bag on him up to the waist and then hovered over him.

"You're the doctor. So treat him," said Joe.

"I never said I was a doctor." She shifted her weight from one foot to the other as tension filled the space.

Say something.

Hollis feared their ruse would be found out, and she would be killed immediately if she didn't sound like she knew what she was talking about.

She lifted her chin. "I'll need to disinfect the wound." She turned to face Joe. "Do you have anything that would work for that? Alcohol will do in a pinch."

He said a prayer of thanks that she could think on her feet. She'd found a way to get Joe out of the room.

"I have some of that. Holler if she tries anything, Derrick."

"I will," said Hollis.

The woman sat down on the cot beside him, so her head was turned away from Joe. Her eyebrows pinched together as though she was trying to ask a question without speaking.

Joe stomped across the damaged wood floor toward the other side of the building, where he'd set up his own sleeping area in another room.

Knowing he had only minutes to talk to the woman in private before Joe came back, Hollis mustered all his strength. If any of their conversation was overheard, he knew the outcome.

They would both be dead.

TWO

The man with the gentle voice grabbed Laura's shirt at the collar and pulled her close. "I'm Hollis Pryce with the FBI."

It took her a second to process the information. Now his sparing her made sense. "Are you investigating the robberies?"

"No time to talk. You have to get away. Only one set of keys to the van. Soldier keeps them on his belt."

She shook her head. "How will I lift them without getting caught?"

"He takes the belt off when he sleeps."

"When is that going to happen?" The situation seemed impossible. From the looks of it, Joe was going to be watching her all the time.

She heard pounding footsteps. Joe was on his way back.

"Prolong my medical treatment. It'll keep you alive."

Joe returned holding a bottle that contained

clear liquid. He held the gun in his other hand and pointed it at her.

Laura rose to her feet, trying to look nonchalant. Hopefully, Joe didn't suspect anything. If they found out who Hollis really was, he'd be shot, too. Her line about needing alcohol for disinfectant had been a wild guess based on the movies she'd watched. She had no idea how to treat a bullet wound.

She turned and faced Hollis so she partially blocked Joe's view.

Hollis touched the bloody patch on his pectoral muscle and mimed using scissors.

"I'm going to need to cut away the fabric around the wound." She hoped she sounded authoritative.

"I have a pocketknife. Here, take this." Joe handed her the bottle of alcohol, which she placed on the floor by the cot. He reached toward his front jeans pocket.

Hollis spoke up. A patina of sweat glistened on his forehead. He was still in a lot of pain. "There's a first-aid kit in my backpack. Should be scissors in there."

"Now why didn't you say you had a first-aid kit earlier?" Anger instantly permeated Joe's voice. "I wouldn't have to have gotten my vodka. I'm sure you have disinfectant in there."

"We're going to need a lot of disinfectant."

Laura hoped that explanation was enough to calm Joe down. For someone to go from zero to sixty on the rage scale like that was a little scary.

Laura rubbed her arms. The cold was starting to get to her.

"You can have the coat by my backpack," said Hollis.

She moved to where the backpack sat propped against the wall and slipped into the coat, feeling instantly warmer. The coat smelled like woodsmoke. She reached for the backpack.

Joe strode across the floor. "Oh, no, you don't. Derrick probably has extra firepower in there." He leaned over and pulled back the toggle on the drawstring. After rifling through the main compartment of the backpack, Joe pulled out a metal container with a first-aid sign on it. He handed it to her.

Still shaking from Joe's volatile reaction earlier, she flipped open the kit and found the scissors. Hollis had slipped one arm out of his coat. She sat on the edge of the cot and looked down at the thermal T-shirt that had been light blue before being stained with blood.

Every time he took in a sharp breath through his teeth, she winced. She'd never been very medically minded. There was a reason she liked computers. "I wish I had something to give you for the pain. Maybe some of the vodka?"

"There should be a pill pack in the kit. Would you look, Joe?"

Still training the gun on Laura, Joe flipped open the first-aid kit. He handed her a packet. "There's a few more packets in here if you need them. Don't know how many pills are in each."

Laura tensed. This was hard enough without having a gun pointed at her. She took the packet, which was labeled Combat Pill Pack. The medications were listed below that. The only name she recognized was Tylenol. She ripped it open. There were five pills inside.

"There's a water bottle at the head of my bed on the floor." Hollis lifted his head.

After getting the water bottle, she placed the pills on his tongue one at a time, offering him a sip of water after each. His brown eyes locked into hers each time, communicating gratitude.

Then she picked up the scissors and cut away enough of the fabric to peel it back from his pectoral muscle. She pressed her lips together so as not to react to the deep, bloody gash. It looked like the wound continued across his shoulder.

Joe, who had been looking over her shoulder, dry heaved and stepped away. "Man, that is nasty."

"You've lost a lot of blood." The smell made her dizzy.

"The bullet caught me as I was turning."

Hollis, who seemed unphased, lifted his shirt-sleeve. "The bullet isn't lodged in muscle. It only grazed me."

"That is good news. So…we just need to deal with that gash. Do you have something in your first-aid kit for that?" She was only guessing at what the next thing to do was.

"Pour some alcohol on it and close it up. What are you waiting for?" Joe had taken two more steps back and put his hand over his mouth. All the color had drained from his face.

The only one with a weaker stomach than her was Joe.

She reached for the first-aid kit, not even sure what she was looking for. She angled the kit so Hollis could see what she was touching and her back obstructed Joe's view. She put her fingers on several packages before Hollis raised his eyebrows, communicating that she had what she needed—a square packet that said Hemostatic Gauze.

Joe continued to make noises indicating his stomach was upset.

Maybe there was a way to get him to leave the room again. "Joe, I'm going to need your help closing this up."

"Oh, no, you're not going to get me to touch that." Joe ran from the room. She could hear him just outside, throwing up.

Despite how dire the situation was, Joe's reaction made her smile.

Hollis grabbed her arm. "After you dress the wound, say that it takes forty-eight hours to make sure there's no infection. Hopefully, that will buy you time. One of the pills I took is an antibiotic. What you're holding in your hand will stop the bleeding, but first you need to clean the wound then pack the gauze in there."

"How do I do that?"

"Just use a little bit of the alcohol on it. That's the quickest way." Hollis grimaced, indicating that he was still in pain.

She lifted the bottle from the floor and poured it on the wound. Once the blood was cleared, the wound didn't look as bad, but it was still a pretty deep cut. More blood seeped out.

"Open the packet. I'll put it in place," said Hollis.

She handed him the gauze. "Now what?"

"Apply some pressure. The bleeding should stop after a few minutes, then get a bandage from the kit to cover it."

She pressed her hand on the gauze feeling his chest rise as he took a deep breath. When she looked into his eyes, her heart fluttered in a way that had nothing to do with the tension of the situation. Until now, she hadn't noticed that he was good-looking in a rugged sort of way.

His Adam's apple moved up and down and then he looked off to the side. "The cut on my arm is not that bad. Just some disinfectant and a bandage should do it."

She searched the medical kit until she found a packet of Neosporin. She ripped it open and applied it to the cut on his upper arm.

Outside, Joe had stopped throwing up. She glanced over her shoulder, expecting to see Joe return with his gun. No sign of him, though.

She turned back to Hollis. "When does Soldier sleep?"

"When he's tired. He doesn't keep a schedule. You may have to wait until dark. I'm not sure what's going to happen since we didn't get anything from the robbery. We were supposed to get orders as to when and where to do a drop after we took our cut." Hollis lifted his head, and his expression changed.

She had not heard his footsteps this time, but Joe must be back in the room. Though her back was to the door, Hollis had a view of the entrance.

She turned slightly to see Joe take up a position at the far end of the room. He was pale except for the intense red splotches on his cheekbones.

Joe shouted from across the room. "What's taking you so long?"

"Almost done," she said. She opened the

package the bandage was in and placed it on Hollis's shoulder.

Exhausted, Hollis eased back on the pillow and closed his eyes. Laura bolted to her feet and turned to face Joe. "I'm going to need to monitor him to make sure he doesn't get an infection."

"How long will that take?"

"At least forty-eight hours. Infection could set in at any time. I could use a chair and some water. Maybe something to eat and the same for Derrick. He needs to keep up his strength."

"How soon will he be well enough to be on the move?"

"Hard to say," said Laura.

Joe's concern over Hollis seemed genuine.

"Let me go talk to Branson and see what he wants to do." Joe looked directly at her. "I don't think he wants to keep you around for too long. I'm sure we'll pull out as soon as we know what the plan is."

Joe pivoted and exited the room.

Laura didn't need such a brutal reminder that she was living on borrowed time.

Hollis felt so weak, he struggled to keep his eyes open. The painkiller paired with the trauma to his body made him tired.

The second Joe was out of the room, the dark-haired woman turned her attention back to him. "Are you okay?"

"Just. Worn. Out." He took a breath between each word. Given the threat Joe had left with, he was amazed that her first concern was about him. "What's your name?"

"Laura."

"Laura," he repeated, noticing the curve of her mouth and the light in her eyes. "I always liked that name."

Pink rose up in her cheeks. It was her turn to look away and stare at the floor.

What was he thinking? This was not the junior high dance. Her life was at stake.

He had so many other questions to ask her. Why had she been in the bank that morning and what had she been doing in that room? He didn't believe that she was a new hire. But helping her escape had to be his priority. He hated that he was so incapacitated. What if Joe came back in a few minutes with the news that Laura had outlived her usefulness? "In my backpack, side pocket, is a pistol. Take it out and put it under my pillow so I can reach it quickly if I need to."

She nodded and grabbed the backpack, slipping the gun under his pillow once she found it. "I don't think there is any way I can get those keys. Joe is probably going to be watching us the whole time. We drove for a long time. Are there any other houses close by? Any way I could find help?"

"Not that I saw." She was right. Not only would she have to try to escape under Joe's guard, but she would also have to hope it was at a time when she could steal the van keys unnoticed. "Do you know how to hot-wire a car?"

She shook her head.

Joe returned. His footsteps sounding like a funeral dirge. Laura whirled around on the cot. Hollis could see that she was so tense, her shoulders nearly touched her ears. She rose to her feet.

Joe held a bottle. "Here's some water."

She took the water bottle. "Thank you."

"Branson wants to know what the signs of infection are."

Her free hand opened and closed nervously. "Why does he need to know? I can take care of him."

"Jury's still out on that." Joe walked across the floor, disappearing into the side room, where he kept his stuff.

She whirled around to Hollis. "What are the signs of infection?"

"Fever, redness and discharge from the wound," said Hollis.

Joe returned with a folding chair. He tossed

what looked like two granola bars on the cot and pulled a third one out of his shirt pocket. His gun, Hollis noticed now, was in a shoulder holster. Joe pointed toward the fireplace and then looked at Laura. "You can take a seat over there after you build a fire to warm this place up."

She stepped over to the fireplace, where logs had been stacked, along with some twigs and paper in a cardboard box.

Joe brushed his hand over his gun before settling down in the chair and watching her with a threatening gaze.

After she had the fire going, Laura picked up the two granola bars and handed one to Hollis.

"The floor is mighty uncomfortable," Hollis said. "You can sit on the edge of the cot if you like. That all right with you, Joe?" The one thing working in their favor was that Joe looked up to Hollis. The kid was barely nineteen but smart enough to realize how unsafe Branson and Soldier were. Hollis had managed to form a tentative bond with the younger man.

Joe responded by shrugging his shoulders.

She nodded. Laura was in such as state of terror that he could see her rapid heartbeat pulsate in her neck. The cot barely shook when she sat down on the end of it. His heart went out to her. He was used to action and violence, but this poor woman clearly was not. He was amazed at how well she'd held it together so far.

She opened the granola bar and took a nibble. After taking a drink of water herself, she offered some to Hollis from his water bottle, holding it for him so he could sip.

The cool liquid felt good going down his throat. He gripped the granola bar. He didn't feel like eating.

Hollis fought to stay awake, as he knew that he had to look for the chance to get Laura to safety. Maybe he could lead her out, hot-wire the car and then claim that she had taken his gun and held him at gunpoint. That ought to preserve his cover.

Joe crossed his arms and watched the two of them. Minutes after his eyes closed, his head fell forward. Then he jerked awake, shook his head, stood up and began pacing.

Despite trying to stay awake, fatigue overtook Hollis as his eyelids became heavy and the fog of sleep made his body go limp.

He awoke in darkness. He had been out for so long, it was nighttime. Laura was gone. And Joe's chair was empty. Fearing the worst, he gathered all his strength, swung his feet to the floor and grabbed the gun from underneath the pillow.

It took substantial effort to get to his feet. He grabbed his flashlight from his backpack. Pain made him shudder when he straightened his spine. Snoring coming from Joe's quarters told him that the younger man must have crawled into bed to sleep. Laura must have taken her chances and sought a way to escape. The other possibility that Soldier or Branson had come and dragged her out to be executed was not one he wanted to think about. He doubted he would have slept through something like that. Once he stepped outside, he noted that the van hadn't been moved.

Not daring to turn on the flashlight, Hollis hurried toward the cabin where Soldier was bunking. He could hear the man muttering to himself and stomping around. No chance that Laura would have been able to get the keys.

When he checked the cabin where Branson should have been, it was empty. Frantic, he searched the area until he noticed light coming from a structure that was set apart from the rest of the buildings. Was Branson down there for some reason?

Then he saw a shadow moving from one tree to the next. It was Laura heading toward the lighted building.

Branson shouted, and a gunshot made him

fear the worst. Despite the pain that stabbed his shoulder, he ran faster.

Dear God, let Laura still be alive.

THREE

Laura sprinted toward the thicket of trees, hoping that would hide her from view. The gunshot had terrified her. Branson wasn't even looking in her direction. He must have sensed her presence and taken the shot when she ran.

A moment before, when she'd looked in on him, Branson had some sort of satellite phone set up and had been talking to a man on a tablet screen. The little bit of conversation she'd heard revealed that Branson was having to explain to the other man what had gone wrong with the robbery.

Once Joe had wandered off to sleep in his room, she'd taken the opportunity to figure out a way to escape, knowing that Hollis would make an excuse for her if Joe woke up. When she passed by his sleeping quarters, Soldier had been wide-awake. If she couldn't escape in the van, she'd hoped to see lights somewhere that indicated other people lived within walking distance.

She'd been drawn to the light in a building down a hill that was set off from the other buildings. There was a lake not too far from the structure. Several rickety old boats and kayaks littered the area around the little building. She hadn't realized then that the light was Branson making his phone call.

Heart pounding, Laura snuck deeper into the trees as Branson stomped by holding a flashlight in one hand and a gun in the other. He shouted up the hill. "What are you doing out here?"

At first, she had thought the comment was directed at her, but then she heard Hollis's voice.

"I heard a gunshot," Hollis said.

"The woman was out snooping around. Joe was supposed to be on guard. After that stunt he pulled in the bank for a few bucks, I've about had it with him."

"Don't fault him. He's a good kid. It's been a hard day for all of us."

"Fine, I won't waste energy punishing him. It's that woman who has me riled. She won't get far on foot if she thinks she can escape," Branson said.

Laura shuddered at the rage in Branson's voice. She was starting to understand that he was the kind of man you didn't cross or betray in even the smallest way.

"You doing all right? You're up and walking, I see." Branson's tone was more accusatory than sympathetic. As if he thought Hollis had faked his injury.

"Gonna be a while before I'm a hundred percent. She did a good job patching me up, though."

"I don't want her around. If you find her, shoot her. We got more important fish to fry."

Laura put a hand over her mouth to stifle a scream. Now she had no choice. She had to find a way to get out of here. Though she hadn't had time for a thorough look, there had been no other lights anywhere, not even across the lake. The hideout was completely isolated.

"Sounds good," said Hollis. "I'll look around here if you want to rally the other two to search."

She heard retreating footsteps. She couldn't see anything but the trees in front of her. How long would it take for Branson to be out of earshot?

She thought she heard footsteps but couldn't be sure. Crouching, she moved closer to the edge of the forest. She saw a figure from the back, probably Hollis. When she looked the other way, a flash of light indicated that Branson was headed up the hill, but was still close enough to turn around and see her if she ran out and tried to get Hollis's attention.

She waited. At first, all she heard was the

lapping of the lake against the shore. Then the sound of two men shouting at each other up the hill filled the silence. Branson must have gotten Soldier motivated, much to his objection.

This was the last place she'd been seen. What if Soldier was sent down this way to look for her, too? When she turned, she saw light closer to the boathouse. Hollis was looking for her in the wrong place.

As fast as she could move without making noise, she hurried toward him. She wouldn't be able to get a clear view unless she stepped away from the trees, but she couldn't risk it, not when a light bobbed from up the hill, indicating one of the others was headed this way.

Staying as close to the trees as she could, she inched closer to the boathouse until a flash of light caused her to dive down behind one of the boats.

Footsteps stomped close to where she was. She pressed her stomach harder against the ground. Who was close? It could be Hollis or Soldier.

She waited a few minutes before lifting her head above the rim of the boat. No lights, no voices. Nothing. She sat up, studying her surroundings while her heart pounded. She was able to make out a figure standing by the water's edge moving his flashlight slowly. Soldier. While his back was to her, she slipped inside the boathouse, thinking she could figure out how to call for help on the device Branson had set up. It was hard to see with only the moonlight illuminating the inside of the boathouse. She felt around. It looked like Branson must have taken the tablet and phone with him. Only the docking station and the power source were left. The antennae must be on the roof. Of course, Branson wouldn't leave everything in place so anyone could use it.

Someone walked by outside. She scooted toward a dark corner and pressed against the wall, praying that he didn't look inside. Soldier grunted and cursed when he slammed into something.

Her breath hitched as she waited and several minutes passed without hearing anything. She moved to peer out a window. The bobbing light told her that someone, probably Soldier, was still close, but not so close that she couldn't make it to the trees, which were a better hiding place. She rose and slipped out the door.

She was only a few feet into the forest when she slammed against what seemed like a wall, but there was a groan. She gasped before she realized she'd run into Hollis. She must have hit his wound when she'd hit him. She shuddered at the thought of causing him pain.

Wrapping his arm around her waist, Hollis pulled her deeper into the trees. "Quiet."

Soldier shouted as he drew closer. "Find anything?"

He must have spotted Hollis's flashlight. Hiding behind Hollis, Laura sunk back into the dark of the forest.

"No, nothing here," said Hollis. "I'll keep looking."

"Orders are just to shoot her when we find her."

Hollis grunted a reply that drowned out her sharp intake of breath.

Hollis remained still, probably deeming that it wasn't safe to talk to her yet. When the other man's flashlight disappeared, he turned to her. "Up the hill, to the van. We don't have much time."

He clicked off the flashlight and took her hand, leading her through the trees. Was this the new plan, that he would hot-wire the van so she could get away? As they worked their way through the forest, she heard shouting and saw lights from time to time.

Then everything fell silent.

He guided her through the trees. She was having a hard time orienting herself. When they came to the edge of the forest, though, she had a clear view of the van and the big building where Hollis and Joe had bunked. She leaned forward and lifted her foot, prepared to make a run for the van. Hollis caught her and pulled her back.

Joe circled around the van holding his gun. Of course, he'd been put on patrol duty to watch the van.

Hollis faced her. He raised his hand and mouthed the word *stay*.

He stepped out from the shelter of the trees. "Hey, Joe."

Laura crouched but lifted her head so she could see Hollis's back.

"Branson said you were helping," Joe replied. "Any sign of her?"

"Nah, I been all through the forest and down by the lake," Hollis said.

"She's got to be somewhere around here. Only a dummy would think they could get away on foot." The tone of Joe's voice became more sympathetic. "You doin' all right?"

"Still a little worn out. Some pain," said Hollis. "How about I get the easy duty watching the van and you can go search west of camp? I don't think that part has been covered."

"Sure, no problem. I heard you saved my bacon with Branson about falling asleep on guard duty. Thanks for having my back."

Laura counted to five before Hollis made an appearance and waved her out with a frantic gesture. "Hurry." He sprinted toward the driver's side of the van.

She got into the passenger seat.

Hollis pulled wires out from underneath the dashboard. "I'll get this started and then you need to scoot over and drive as fast as you can."

She glanced out the front window. "Got it. How are you guys going to get out of here?"

"I think Branson has communication resources he didn't disclose, judging from what I saw in that boathouse."

"I saw that, too. He was talking to someone on a tablet screen."

Hollis's hands stilled for a moment. "You saw the guy?"

"Just for a second."

He continued to work, pressing two wires together. The van sparked to life. His hand was on the door when he glanced up through the windshield. Soldier was stalking toward them, gun in hand. His gaze was fixed on Hollis.

Hollis's jaw dropped. "My cover's blown. Looks like I'm going with you."

Laura let out a gasp as Soldier ran toward them, raised his gun and fired.

Heart pounding, Hollis pressed the gas and jerked the wheel. Pain zinged in his shoulder, radiating through his whole body and making even his teeth hurt. He wasn't in any condition to drive, but he had no choice.

He pressed the gas pedal and turned in a wide

arc. Backing up would have taken too much time. He heard the pinging of gunfire but kept driving. The van rattled and shook as they rounded the first curve, the headlights illuminating the patchy road. Accelerating, he felt the van sputter and jerk. He hoped it was just the roughness of the road—otherwise he feared one of the bullets had damaged the engine.

They had no choice but to keep going.

He drove for another five minutes before steam rolled out of the hood and the van quit all together. There was no time to mourn the situation. Soldier probably knew that the engine would give out and was on his way toward them.

Hollis knew they had only one choice. They'd have to walk out of the woods, despite his weakened state. But there was nothing in the vehicle that would be useful for their survival. All he had was his gun and five bullets.

Laura gazed at him with an expression that seemed to say *what now?*

"We've got to hoof it out. But we won't last without supplies in winter weather. We need to circle back and get the stuff in my backpack."

Laura shook her head in disbelief. "Go back? They'll kill us if they catch us."

Hollis reached for the door handle. "It's the best option. It's probably twelve hours of hiking in winter weather and that's if we can stick to the road."

"I'm just afraid, is all." She ran her fingers through her long dark hair.

"I'm sure this is way more than you bargained for as a bank teller."

"I'm not a bank teller. Angela said that to save my life. I'm a computer-security expert hired by First Federal to beef up security because of the other robberies. Looks like I was a day late in getting there."

He reached over and squeezed her hand. "I'm sorry you have to go through this, but we don't have much time."

She nodded and pushed open the door. Once he came around to her side of the van, he led them off the road and into the copse of trees. They went deep enough into the forest so they wouldn't be seen from the road.

After they'd hiked only a short distance, exhaustion overtook him, and he pressed his back to a tree and lowered himself to the ground. What he really needed was to be resting on his cot for a day or two in order to recover from the trauma of the gunshot wound. Laura sat down facing him, her features etched with compassion.

"Is there anything I can do?"

"Just let me catch my breath and rest for a bit." Each inhale caused a new stab of pain.

She glanced in the direction they had just come, probably wondering if they would be followed. He had no idea what kind of tracking skills Soldier had. The little bit he'd been able to learn about the man was that he was basically a mercenary who had done some jail time. In his brief conversations with Soldier, it was clear that the man had no ties to any other human being and really no permanent home.

Hollis closed his eyes. "He'll probably head down the road for a bit before he figures out we went deeper into the trees. For sure, he won't be expecting us to return to camp."

"I'll let you rest. I'm going to have a look around."

"I only need a few minutes to get my strength back." He wasn't so sure that was true, but he didn't want to scare Laura even more.

"I won't go far," she said.

He listened to her walk away. Hollis closed his eyes and prayed that he would have the fortitude to get himself, and Laura, back to civilization.

He said over and over, "I can do all things through Christ who strengthens me."

The pain that wracked his body told another story. But he had to fight through it or he and Laura would not be able to escape.

FOUR

Laura walked a wide arc around where Hollis was resting. She hadn't wanted him to see how badly her hands were shaking. It was clear that he was in no condition to keep running and dodging gunfire. He needed rest and time to heal.

Though she could not see much in the dark, she studied the landscape. Nothing but trees and fallen logs in every direction. They had only made it a couple of turns down the mountain in the van, so they couldn't be that far from the camp. How long would it be before Soldier and the others figured out that they hadn't tried to follow the road down, but were headed back to camp?

She walked toward the tree where Hollis was. She heard him even before she stood face-to-face with him. He kept repeating the same thing.

"I can do all things through Christ, who strengthens me."

It took her a second to realize it was a Bible verse. She vaguely remembered it, or at least one that sounded similar. As a child, her father had dropped her off at endless vacation Bible schools during the summer. Not because he had deep religious convictions, but because it was free day care for a single dad who didn't have much money to spare. Her mother had died shortly after she was born.

"Sorry, you caught me praying."

She shrugged. "Do what you want. I prefer to rely on something more concrete."

"Guess we have a difference of opinion on that."

A noise closer to the road interrupted their conversation. Hollis staggered to his feet, still leaning his back against the trunk for support. She whirled around, scanning the trees but not seeing anything.

"We better get moving. Just in case." He had pushed away from the tree but still rested his hand there.

"Let me help you." She slipped in under his good arm and supported him as he walked. Her hand wrapped around his waist. His heavy breathing indicated how hard moving uphill was for him. They hiked for another five minutes before she helped him get down on the ground to rest. Sweat had formed on his forehead.

"Are you going to be okay?"

He said nothing, just studied her for a long moment.

"Don't sugarcoat it," she urged him. "Just tell me the truth."

"I think if I could get a few hours' sleep, I'd be up to the task at hand."

She kneeled beside him and wiped the sweat from his brow. His skin felt warm beneath her fingers. She wasn't the medical expert, but she had a feeling he needed a few days' rest and probably some more pain medication.

At least, there wasn't much snow on the ground. All the same, it seemed to be getting colder.

Before zipping the coat Hollis had loaned her, she stared down at the orange-and-blue floral pattern of her blouse and her navy wool slacks. This morning, when she'd chosen her business-casual outfit and left her hotel room for the bank, felt like a hundred years ago. How had her predictable life changed so radically? She wondered if she would ever get back to her quiet apartment where she lived alone. Days off spent reading and sitting in the park felt like a dream right now compared to the nightmare she had been pulled into.

"I'm ready to go," said Hollis.

His voice sounded stronger. Always, it held

that warm gentle quality that had clued her in that he wasn't a hardened criminal. The one thing she was grateful for was that Hollis was here with her. He clearly had more training and skills than she had. And he had blown his cover to try to save her.

They trekked uphill a few hundred yards.

Through the trees, she saw some sort of structure. The white of the walls contrasted with the dark forest. "What is that building?"

"Not sure. It looks like it's made of concrete."

She still couldn't see any of the cabins of the camp. This building was set off from the rest of the resort.

They stepped closer toward the structure. Some faded graffiti adorned the cracked white concrete exterior walls. One of the walls was crumbling. Inside, it looked like the building had been some sort of pump house, judging from the metal pipes sticking out of the wall and scattered on the floor.

"Let's go in here. You can rest. It'll be a little warmer."

She helped him to the floor. He propped his back against the wall, and she sat beside him. Through the roof, which had partially deteriorated to the point that there was a gaping hole, she could see the stars. She listened to the intensity of his breathing.

"You need to stay here. You're still really weak. I'll go into the camp alone and get what we need. Just tell me what to grab."

He didn't answer for a long moment. "You know how to use a gun?"

The idea made her shudder. "No. Keep the gun. You'll need it to protect yourself…just in case. It would just be a liability in my hands."

"I could hang back and watch, be a lookout for you. If it came to it, I would use my gun."

She weighed their options. Some protection and an extra pair of eyes would reduce the fear she felt at having to do such a dangerous act. If they had to run in a hurry, though, Hollis would not be able to keep up. "I don't know what to do."

They sat together for a long moment in the dark. Hollis tilted his head and gazed at the stars. "I need to pray. If that's all right?"

"If you want to." She had been a bit abrupt with him earlier when she'd heard him praying. There had been a time when, as a child who didn't have a mom or siblings, she'd prayed to God to end her loneliness. By the time she was a teenager, she'd found computers and books to be much more dependable than God, Who seemed to have lost her address.

"God, we need Your help. We need to know what to do. We need Your protection."

Hollis had a very soothing voice. She wasn't used to someone praying in such a sincere and vulnerable way.

He ended the prayer and continued to stare at the night sky. Even with the danger that lay ahead, being this close to him and feeling his shoulder press against hers was a comfort.

She cleared her throat. "How far do you think we are from the rest of the buildings?"

"Not sure. I didn't even know this building was here."

"What do we need to get from the camp?"

"Those pill packets and some food from my backpack. There should be a thermal blanket in there, too. We can't just grab my backpack. They'll notice it missing and figure out we came back."

Hollis was taking a breath between each word, which meant he was still in a lot of pain. The guy was so selfless, he'd probably want to help even if he had a broken leg.

"What do we have—four or five hours before daylight? Why don't we both rest for an hour or so?"

Hollis laughed but stopped abruptly and grimaced. Poor guy. It probably hurt to laugh. "I'm not falling for that. You were going to sneak off while I slept."

How had he guessed she was thinking that? "Hollis, you're in a lot of pain."

"I've been through worse. I'd sleep a lot better if I had some painkillers and something soft for my head." He pushed himself to his feet. "We've rested enough. Let's get going. You can get the essentials out of my backpack. I'll hang back and watch."

Arguing with him was pointless. She stepped out of the building, moving with caution because it was hard to gauge the terrain in the darkness. Hollis remained several feet behind her but kept up. The smell of a fire burning indicated they must be getting close to camp. And then she heard loud rock music.

She slowed down even more. The metal roof of the main structure glinted in the moonlight. One of the men, she couldn't tell who, had built a fire on the road between the main building and the other cabins. He sat in a folding chair with his music blasting. As she drew closer, she saw that he was hunched forward, probably sleeping. Judging from the man's build, it was Joe.

She crouched down and waited for Hollis to catch up. He was out of breath when he moved in beside her. "The front entrance is being watched. Is there a back door to where your stuff is?"

He nodded and then cupped his hand on her shoulder. "This way. I'm right behind you."

She glanced back down at the resort. There were no other lights on anywhere. Were the other men still out looking for them, or had they gone to sleep? It seemed odd that Joe had been put on some kind of watch duty. Why not use all the available manpower to find them?

Laura took in a breath and headed down toward the back of the big building. She found the entrance easily enough. It was a bare threshold where a door used to be. When she stepped over it, she was in a dark hallway. She headed toward where she saw a doorway, hoping that the building layout wasn't so complex that she would not be able to find the room where Hollis had stored his stuff.

The floor creaked as she walked across it. She was grateful Joe was playing his music so loud. Moonlight shone through the holes in the ceiling, and she was able to navigate to Hollis's cot.

The first-aid kit had been left out. Unable to read the tiny labels, she gathered all the packets of pills and put them in her pocket. She unzipped the first compartment of the backpack and pulled out a large plastic container that said it was an MRE, a freeze-dried meal that the army used in the field. She also found two granola bars. She located the package that contained the thermal blanket and stuffed it in another coat pocket. Hollis's small pillow was mostly hidden by his sleeping bag. It probably wouldn't be missed. She grabbed it, along with the water bottle by the bed. Then she moved toward the hallway, preparing to exit the same way she'd come in.

The sound of a car engine outside caused her to do an about-face. She saw headlights and heard voices. She moved closer toward the entrance, pressing against the wall, and peered out. There were two men talking to Joe. Men she hadn't seen before.

Fear gripped her heart, making it hard to breathe.

It looked like Branson had called in reinforcements and gotten another vehicle. She pressed her back against the wall and listened.

One of the men spoke up. "This whole thing is a disaster. Let's get organized and make sure those two don't get off this mountain alive."

Laura bolted for the back door.

Hollis knew something was wrong the minute Laura stepped outside. Though he couldn't see her expression clearly, her body language—the stiffness of her movements and the glancing from side to side—told him they were in trouble. He thought he had heard an engine running but it was hard to discern above the music.

He stood up from his hiding place as she sprinted toward him. "What is it?"

"They got two more guys and another car."

It felt like a rock had just been thrown against his stomach. He purged the fear from his voice before speaking. The most contagious thing in the world was panic. "They're going to be looking for us down the mountain. We rest up and then move out behind them."

The plan was risky no matter what. The men could double back.

She nodded. Had the men left yet? The rock music was still playing. But maybe Joe was still standing guard.

"Let's head back to that pump house. It's pretty well hidden."

They worked their way uphill. Hollis gazed down at the front part of the camp. The music had grown fainter in the distance, but Joe still had the fire going. Unless they did a wide arc around the camp, there was no way they could get to that communication station Branson had set up. Knowing Branson, he'd probably taken the key components with him so it wouldn't work, anyway. The guy was smart. He was the one that Hollis had been able to learn almost nothing about. And now, from what Laura had said, Branson appeared to be in direct communication with the man who was the mastermind behind the robberies.

Hollis had no idea if Branson had family,

what his former profession was or if he even had a permanent home somewhere. In many ways, he was the most dangerous man in the group. Soldier had no qualms about being violent, but he wasn't smart like Branson.

Hollis leaned over, resting his hands on his knees. Because of the dark and not wanting to draw attention to themselves, they were going at a snail's pace up the hill. But now, even light exertion exhausted him.

"You want some help?" Laura's voice was filled with anxiety.

In many ways, he was a liability to her. He hated being the weak link in anything he did, let alone when his and Laura's lives were on the line.

"I'll be all right. Maybe I should take that painkiller. It'll kick in about the time I can rest."

She pulled a handful of pill packets out of her pockets. "I didn't know which ones would work so I grabbed everything."

He sorted through the pile, ripped open the container and swallowed the pills.

As they hiked the remaining distance, Laura veered closer to him, standing on his good side. She probably wanted to be able to help him if he needed it.

He was relieved to see the crumbling pump house.

"Do you have a pocketknife?" she asked.

"Sure, what do you need it for?"

"I can cut down some tree boughs and maybe make a little softer bed for you than the concrete floor."

He handed her the knife, and she gave him the pillow, which she had stuffed in her coat. Exhausted, he crawled into the pump house and propped himself against a wall. Laura returned several times with an armful of evergreen boughs.

She talked as she arranged the branches. "I suppose one of us should keep watch." She lifted her hand. "I nominate me."

If laughing didn't hurt so much, he would have had a good chuckle over her quick wit. "You can use the thermal blanket to keep warm."

She had pulled the index-card-size packet out of one of her pockets. "I think you need it more than me."

He lifted the pillow. "I have the pillow and the branches." He crawled onto the makeshift bed, which, he had to admit, was an improvement over a cold concrete floor. "What made you think of cutting down the tree boughs?"

"My father and I used to go camping a lot. He liked roughing it, building a lean-to and stuff, so he taught me." She tore open the Mylar blanket and placed it over his legs.

The comment was a reminder that Laura was a person with a life. "Your dad still alive?"

"No. Except for some relatives I've only met a couple of times, he was my only family. My mom died when I was a baby." She took up a position at the open threshold.

He recognized the note of sadness that entered her voice.

"I'm sure when you went to work this morning, you didn't think the day would end up this way," he said.

She scoffed. "I'm used to the predictability of computers and security systems. I like quiet things like museums and reading in a cozy."

He patted the tree branches. "You have some camping skills."

"I guess that makes me not a total nerd." She drew her knees up toward her chest.

He rested his head on the pillow. "Sorry that you have to go through all of this."

"I saw how hard you tried to get them to leave me behind. I do appreciate that."

"We didn't count on you being in that bank," Hollis said. "I imagine someone is worried about you about now."

"Not really. I travel a lot for my job all over the state. I checked in to a hotel last night for this job. I don't even have a cat. All I have is an aloe vera named George. He's very low-maintenance."

He wondered why someone who was clearly such a good person would be so detached from life. There was probably a story there. As he adjusted the pillow underneath his head, he wished that he and Laura had met under different circumstances.

Her remarks about his praying suggested that she did not share his faith.

At the very least, they could have been friends. None of that seemed possible considering the nightmare that had thrown them together.

"So where did you get your medical knowledge?"

"I was a medic in the army before I joined the Bureau."

"You like exciting jobs."

"Yes, I like unpredictability. Keeps me on my toes." He let out a breath. "Guess that makes me the opposite of you."

"For sure."

The medication had alleviated much of the pain and he drifted off.

At some point, he must have moaned in his sleep. As he woke up, Laura made a shushing sound and touched his forehead lightly. "I have another pain pill here for you." On autopilot, he opened his mouth and swallowed the pill. Barely cognizant, he fell into an even deeper sleep.

He was awakened by Laura's soft touch on

his good shoulder. "One of the new guys came back with the car. I'm going to go closer and see if I can figure out what they're doing. I'll stay hidden. I didn't want you to wake up and not know where I was."

She left before he could even respond and then he drifted off again. Pain caused him to sleep in spurts. When he woke again, he saw that Laura was back. She had fallen asleep in the doorway and was resting her head against the frame.

The stars still twinkled in the night sky and he fell back asleep. The sun was shining on his face the next time he opened his eyes, and Laura was gone.

He got up and moved toward the doorway. It took him a moment to spot Laura as she worked her way up the hill. She sprinted from one hiding spot to another, always glancing over her shoulder twice. As she drew close, he saw the look of utter terror on her face.

FIVE

Laura nearly crashed into Hollis's arms. "We need to get moving. Soldier is coming up this way."

Hollis had some color in his face. The rest had done him good, but how long would it be before he was spent again?

Hollis peered down the hill. Trees would have blocked his view of what she'd seen—Soldier with a rifle, headed this way. She had run as quickly and carefully as she could, but there was no telling if she had been spotted. The fresh tree boughs inside the pump house would give away that they had been here, but there was no time to dispose of them.

They grabbed the water and food, and circled around the concrete structure, heading farther up the hill.

"We can't get too far from the road or we'll get lost," Hollis said. "This way." He placed his hand on her arm and directed her at a slight diagonal.

She wasn't sure where they were in relationship to the road, but Hollis seemed to have a bead on their location.

They walked for at least five minutes. Hollis peered over his shoulder. "Get down."

She dropped to the ground and he slipped in beside her. She saw then that Soldier had closed some of the distance between them. Except for a red bandana around his neck, he blended in with his surroundings. He was moving quickly up the hill.

Beside her, Hollis gasped for breath. He still fatigued easily. There was no way they could outrun Soldier.

Soldier disappeared from view when he went inside the pump house. This was their chance to find a better hiding place. Both of them burst to their feet at the same time and moved toward the thicker part of the forest. They didn't need to exchange words to know what the plan was, because they'd both seen how quickly Soldier could move. They ran for a few minutes more before finding a tree that had fallen down from the roots.

"Too obvious," said Hollis. He kept moving. Soldier would probably only take seconds to glance inside the pump house and conclude that they had been there.

Hollis directed her deeper into the trees and farther away from where he'd said the road was. He tugged on her sleeve, pointing toward a clump of trees. She sunk to her knees and settled in behind one, with her stomach pressed against the trunk so she could peer out in the direction that Soldier probably would be coming.

Hollis pulled his gun from the holster and chose a tree not far from her.

Maybe it had been a mistake to rest through part of the night. The darkness would have hidden them, but Hollis had been in no condition to be on the move. Though he had gotten easily winded once they had taken off running, his features were no longer contorted with pain.

While her heartbeat drummed in her ears, she listened. Though she did not see Soldier at all, there was a sort of muffled pounding that was probably his footsteps. It was hard to tell how far away he was. Her fingers dug into the bark of the tree as her breath caught in her throat.

Hollis jerked and lifted his gun.

She wondered if his vantage point allowed him to see something she couldn't.

He signaled for her to stay put by holding his palm toward her. He sprinted to another tree, crouched and tilted his head sideways to see around the trunk.

Laura tensed as she scanned the area where Hollis was looking, hoping to see a flash of red. The thick foliage revealed nothing. Hollis edged farther away from her.

Just when she feared he would move out of view, he waved for her to come toward him.

She picked a tree midway between them and sprinted toward it with light steps, grateful that the snow was soft. She took in a deep breath. When she looked through the trees, she saw the fragment of red she'd been looking for. Soldier was getting closer to them. That was why Hollis had wanted to move.

As she pressed against the tree and watched, Hollis remained in place as well, probably looking for an opportunity when it would be safe to make a run for it.

Though it felt like eons, she wasn't sure how much time passed while her legs grew stiff from being in a crouching position. She could no longer see the red that indicated where Soldier was, but he must still be too close for comfort if Hollis was not yet ready to move.

She jumped when she heard noises off to the side. Not Soldier, but a different man yelling something. She couldn't discern the words, but now they knew there was a second man close by.

She froze in place, not sure what to do. Crashing noises off to the side, and deadfall being crushed by boots, told her the other man was getting closer. Soldier's voice, clear and distinct, responded to being shouted at.

"Over here, man."

Her heart pounded. Soldier was closer than she'd realized.

Hollis turned and signaled for her to retreat. She headed back in the general direction she'd just been, but at a diagonal angle from where the second man's voice had come from.

Glancing off to the side, she noticed flashes of movement that indicated the second man was close. She prayed the thickness of the foliage would hide her and that Hollis would be able to catch up.

She slipped behind a cluster of trees just as she heard the second man shouting. "Hey, I saw something over here."

The sounds of boots pounding the ground and breaking branches filled the air and grew louder. She'd been spotted. She had no choice but to run flat out. As she headed deeper into the forest, gunfire rang out behind her. One shot. Then another shot from a different gun a second later.

She ran even faster for a few minutes. Out of breath, she slowed her pace. Silence settled behind her.

Had Hollis given up his position to save her by firing a shot? Was he okay, or was he lying on the forest floor bleeding to death?

Breathing heavily, Hollis fell back and hid before Soldier could get a bead on his position and fire another shot. The first shot had been a wild guess. The second man, who had been shouting for Soldier, had come so close to Laura that Hollis had had to do something to stop him. He had lifted his gun and pulled the trigger.

He couldn't tell if the man had been hit or had simply retreated from the gunfire. In any case, the shot had caused the man to stop and given Laura a chance to get away.

Knowing that he could not outrun Soldier, Hollis chose one hiding place after another. Soldier came into view, jaw set like granite, rifle in his hand. The second man, one of the new recruits, a muscular, short bald man, approached Soldier, cupping his hand over his ear. Soldier addressed the bald man, who responded in a shrill, distressed voice. Either Hollis had nicked the man's ear, or the shot had come close enough to his head to damage his hearing.

Hollis took advantage of Soldier being distracted to rush toward another hiding place. He kept moving, crouching and hiding, making his way in the direction Laura had run. The voices behind him intensified. Soldier must be on his tail again. Hollis found a hiding place and waited. Ten yards away, he heard one of the men passing by.

He prayed that Laura would just keep running and not try to come back for him. If he could shake these two men, he'd find her somehow, but he didn't want her put in harm's way.

Hollis waited until he heard retreating footsteps before he dashed for the next hiding place. He continued until the sound of the two men searching for him faded, and then he jogged without stopping. He surveyed the landscape in front of him, hoping to see some sign of where Laura had gone.

There were no clear trails to follow. A few paths, where deer had trod over and over, were evident. Knowing most people tended to move where it was easiest, he chose one of the deer trails and headed through the trees.

Retreating this far meant they had gotten away from the road that would help them navigate back to civilization. When he glanced over his shoulder, he caught glimpses of the bald man, whose bright orange shirt contrasted with the snow and trees. That meant Soldier must be close by, too.

He'd put some distance between himself and the other two men, but not enough to feel safe.

When he looked again at the brush up ahead, Laura popped up her head and then went back down. She must have been waiting and watching for him. After she'd spotted him, she'd taken a chance when she'd stuck up her head above her hiding place.

In his flight, Hollis had headed downhill into a valley. He ran toward where Laura was after glancing over his shoulder. The other two men were at the top of the hill. The serpentine pattern of their walking and the way they glanced around indicated that the pursuers did not know for sure where he'd gone.

Once he got to where Laura was, the foliage was too thick to see the other two men. He slipped in beside Laura.

"I'm glad you found me," she said. Her words held a note of affection. "I was worried about you."

"Thanks for waiting."

"You need a minute to catch your breath?"

He was wheezing a little, but he shook his head. "They're not that far behind. We should keep moving."

"How are we going to get back to the road?"

"I'm not sure. First we've got to shake these guys."

He turned to go, assessing the terrain in front of him—it was populated with thin-trunked lodgepole pine trees. The forest would provide them with a degree of cover.

As they walked at a steady and intense pace, he could feel the fatigue settle into his muscles. His wound started to hurt. He slowed down.

Laura, who had been walking a few feet in front of him, must have sensed something. She turned to face him. "You look really pale. You need to rest."

Her concern touched him deeply.

"No." He dug into his pocket and pulled out one of the pill packets. "Not yet." He took the two pain pills left in the packet.

Laura turned in a half circle, taking in her surroundings. "If we get up to the other side of the valley to that ridge, where we can see more, maybe we can stop to eat some of the food I grabbed."

He estimated that where she was pointing was at least a half-hour hike. He nodded. "Let's do that."

She walked beside him as they made their way through the forest and up the hill. The ridge that looked out on the valley had lots of brush and some rocks. When he looked off to the east, he could see the roof of the main building of the abandoned resort. Because they had been forced to move sideways instead of downhill, they were actually not far from the resort as the crow flew. They weren't making much progress.

He settled on the ground and Laura pulled out a granola bar she'd grabbed from his backpack. "Should we split this?"

"How much food did you get?"

She checked her pockets, pulling out one MRE packet and another granola bar.

It was hard to guess how long it would take to hike over rough terrain before they intersected the road that led into town. Because they'd been driven off track, they still had a substantial walk to get back to where they could see the road. Rationing food made sense. "Yes, why don't we split it?"

She ripped open the package and bent the bar in half. "We're not going to get out of here before dark, are we?"

He shook his head as he took a bite of the granola bar.

"I saw how close we are to the resort still," Laura said.

He took another small bite of the granola bar. Things didn't look good. There were four or five men looking for them. One of them could have driven down to the base of the mountain, where it intersected with the country road, to patrol it and wait for them. Even if they could make it there in the dark, there was no guarantee they

could make it out. Not to mention, he was still
in a lot of pain. The pills helped with that, but
he still got tired easily. And he had only four
more bullets left.

"What if we tried to get that car those other
two men came up in?" Laura asked.

"I doubt they just parked it. They're probably using it to drive up and down the road to
look for us."

"Is there nothing else close by? Maybe on the
other side of that lake? There must be people
around here somewhere." Her voice was filled
with desperation.

"Before the robbery, we had time to dump
our gear and rest up for a few hours before daylight. I didn't see any signs of people or struc-
tures anywhere." He appreciated that she was
trying to problem-solve, but the smart thing to
do would be to head down the mountain the way
they'd come in. Stepping into the unknown of
the surrounding wilderness could only make
their situation worse.

"Do you think the police will come looking
up here?"

"If they were looking, I think we would have
seen a helicopter by now. One thing we did before the robbery was drop a van off by the nearest airport that looks exactly like the one we
drove, so it would appear we fled the state."

"You found out quite a bit about how the operation is planned," she said. "I'm sorry your cover was blown because you were trying to help me."

As he ate the last morsel of food, Hollis fought off the despair that threatened to engulf him. His undercover part in the investigation was over. Though he had not brought it up to Laura, the only thing he felt hopeful about where the investigation was concerned was that Laura had probably seen the man who planned the robberies on that tablet screen. If he could get Laura safely out, she might be able to help break this case. "Maybe we can still solve the case. I just won't be undercover." That realization was not enough to lift his spirits about their current situation. "Do you remember what the guy on the tablet screen, the one Branson was talking to, looked like? He could be the man I am after, the one who has planned the robberies."

"I only got a quick look at him. Maybe if I saw him again, I could identify him."

"What were the two men talking about?"

"I didn't hear much of the conversation." Laura took a last bite of her granola bar. "The tone was pretty heated, and they seemed to be talking about what to do since the robbery had gone wrong."

"But you couldn't say if Branson or the other guy was calling the shots?"

She shook her head. "Not really."

The guy could have just been a go-between, but right now it was the only lead Hollis had. None of it mattered if they didn't get back to civilization.

Hollis lifted himself above the rock to assess the best path to navigate back to the road. That was the exact moment when Soldier and the bald man emerged from the edge of the forest. They had split off in different directions and Soldier was headed right for the ridge where they were hiding.

Hollis dipped down below the rock. "We need to get out of here. Now."

SIX

Laura took a deep breath to try to stave off the rising panic. "They spotted us?"

"Soldier is headed right toward us, and the other guy is searching to the north." Still crouching below the rock and brush, Hollis faced south. "We need to head this way. Stay low."

She tried not to give in to fear. Even if they got away unnoticed from these two men, there were three other very determined men looking for them. She doubted the criminals would give up until they were standing over their lifeless bodies.

Hollis burst out, ran a few yards and settled behind some brush. She followed him, crouching and pressing against his back so the foliage concealed her, though there were not many leaves left on the bush. Only when she was safely hidden did she peer out to try to see where the other two men were. She caught glimpses of Soldier as he headed up toward where they had just been, but she could not see the bald man anywhere.

They ran to another hiding spot.

Shots were fired at them from uphill. The bald man had spotted them.

The bald man shouted, "Over there."

It would only be seconds before Soldier was on their tail as well. They sprinted toward the trees and kept running. Though he seemed winded, Hollis led the way. He chose their path through the forest. The snow was uneven enough to not show a clear trail of where they had gone. She assumed Hollis was navigating back toward the road in a roundabout way. She had to trust his sense of direction because she had no idea where they were going.

They kept moving for at least an hour with no further gunfire, or even any sign that they had been followed.

Hollis slowed down and then collapsed on the ground. He was breathing heavily and pale.

She sat beside him. "Are you okay?"

"I have to be," he said. "We need to keep going."

He was right. The two men couldn't be far behind. She put out a hand for him and helped him to his feet. Hollis directed her to veer east, which probably meant he was trying to get them back close to the road.

As they worked their way down the mountain, the late afternoon turned into early evening. Gray covered the sky. They stayed on the move. Twice, she heard noises behind her that indicated at least one of their pursuers was close.

Because she had been in the back of the van and unable to see as they came up the mountain, Laura had no reference for the landmarks they passed. She had no idea how far down the mountain they'd gone. Hollis continued to walk in a southeast direction, but she still saw no sign of the road.

Hollis was slowing down and having to rest more. He placed one palm on a tree and bent over. It had been some time since they had seen or heard any sign of Soldier or the bald man.

She patted his good shoulder. "Once it gets dark, we can rest and eat some."

He nodded, still trying to catch his breath.

She offered him a swig from the water bottle and then took a drink herself.

As it grew dark, they continued to hike, but much slower. By the time the sky turned black and the stars came out, they were moving at a snail's pace across crunchy snow.

It was clear that Hollis needed to rest. In the dark, it was hard to see anything but the outlines of the trees and a few details of the forest that the moonlight illuminated.

"We should eat, huh?"

He didn't say anything but chose a flat spot on the ground.

She pulled the MRE out of her pocket and angled it so she could read the label. "Looks like lasagna is on the menu."

"Pour some water into that pouch," he said. "And put the main entrée in there. It'll heat it up."

She ripped open the container Hollis had pointed to and poured some water into it, then put the lasagna packet in the plastic mini oven. The big packet contained other food, crackers and a dessert, which they could eat later. She opened the plastic utensils. "You want the fork or the spoon?"

"Fork," Hollis said. "You can have the first bite."

Her growling stomach indicated an intense level of hunger that he must have been feeling as well, yet he was a gentleman and offered her first dibs on the meal. She took several spoonfuls and then passed the food to him. The hot meal warmed her up. Hollis edged back until he could lean against a tree.

He ate quickly and then took a gulp of water.

She scooted in beside him. "I can keep watch if you want to get some shut-eye. Don't argue with me. It's clear to me that you need sleep more than I do."

He laughed. "Wake me in half an hour, so

you can get a nap, too. Then we should move out while it's still dark." Hollis folded his arms and rested his head against the back of the tree.

Within minutes, his breathing changed as he snored softly. If he had been in the military, he was probably used to falling asleep in uncomfortable places.

There was something sweet about the way his head tilted to the side. She had to admit that she liked him. Not something she had felt for a man in a long time. She wondered if they had met under different circumstances if they could have dated. Because of her shyness and the long hours and travel for her job, she had given up on the idea of marriage or even a relationship. As she listened to Hollis's gentle snoring, she found herself wishing her life had gone in a different direction.

She could feel herself about to nod off. To keep from falling asleep, she stood up and paced a circle around where Hollis was. Taking note of the landmarks she could discern in the near darkness, she made an even wider circle. She saw nothing but more trees.

When she stood still and listened, there seemed to be only the creaking of branches. But then she detected another sound, more mechanical in nature. A car maybe. She stepped in the direction she thought the noise had come from but couldn't hear it anymore.

Was it a car that had gone by on the road and fallen out of earshot? If so, the road must still be pretty far away because she had not seen any lights. She retreated back to Hollis.

But he wasn't there.

She did not see him beneath the tree where she thought she'd left him sleeping. She turned slightly, wondering if she'd gotten lost. Her heart thudded as she scanned the darkness.

Two bobbing lights glinted through the trees and then disappeared. Two of the men were coming this way, probably Soldier and the bald man. She turned to run toward where she thought she'd heard the car.

"Hollis," she whispered.

He must have seen the men approaching, too, and was either hiding, or he'd gone searching for her. The lights flashed again and this time the men's voices carried on the night air. Though she could not decipher the exact words, their tone was calm. She took that to mean they hadn't spotted her or Hollis.

Still, she kept moving. She zigzagged through the trees while she searched for Hollis. If he was close, he would hear her. But there was no sign of him.

The terrain changed beneath her, growing

flatter and more even as the trees fell away, until she found herself on a narrow dirt road. Was it the road that led back to safety? She couldn't be sure, but all roads led somewhere.

She followed it for a short distance. It seemed to grow wider.

Behind her, the men began to shout. From the sound of their voices, it seemed as if they were too far away to have spotted her. It must have been Hollis they were after. She sprinted to the other side of the road, seeking the cover of the trees.

As she hid among the dense boughs, the shouting intensified and a dark figure bolted onto the road. Hollis.

She opened her mouth to call out his name just as the headlights of a car engulfed him. He was hemmed in by danger on two sides.

Hollis dashed toward the far side of the road when the car barreled toward him. Running with his last ounce of strength, he pushed his way through the trees. Behind him, car doors slammed, and a cacophony of excited voices filled the air. Then gunfire echoed behind him. It spurred him deeper into the forest. A branch thwacked his head. His shoulder ached.

As he passed a thick tree, a hand slipped into his. Laura had found him. She held on to his hand, giving him the willpower to keep going. Though the men were no longer shouting, he could hear them getting closer.

There was no time to look over his shoulder. The noise indicated that the men were still a threat. For a second or so, a light would bob into his peripheral vision. As Laura led them farther away from the road, he wondered if all the men had gone on the search-and-destroy mission, or if one had stayed with the car. If the car was unguarded, they might be able to get to it and escape. If not, the move might cost them their lives.

As they worked their way through the thick undergrowth, he heard the sound of rushing water. They moved toward it and came upon a river so suddenly that they both tumbled down the steep bank.

He lost his hold on Laura's hand, but she was close enough for him to see her.

There was no alternative. The men were within shooting distance. Going into the icy river in the winter would be a death sentence, so they ran along the river's edge until they reached a cluster of bushes.

Flashlight beams swung across the surface of the water as the men walked along the steep bank.

There was only one light above him now, but

it was close enough to reveal him if one of the criminals aimed the light in the right direction. Hollis dragged himsclf down the rocky shore to the next bit of cover. Laura was a few paces ahead of him. Just as he reached some tall grass, one of the men shouted.

"There—there! I see one of them."

The beam of light hadn't comc ncar him. They must have spotted Laura. He scanned the lighted area but didn't see her. She must have kept moving.

He pressed to the ground, and heard footsteps and grunting behind him. One of the men had come down the steep bank.

Hollis rolled toward the water and lay flat and still as the river lapped against the shore close to his ear.

His focus on Laura, the man stomped by Hollis, coming so close that his passing created a breeze against Hollis's skin.

He closed his eyes and prayed for Laura's safety.

He listened to him move away from the river. The steps were slow and deliberate, which meant he didn't know where Laura had gone.

"I can't see nothing." The voice was Soldier's.

"Keep looking," another voice replied. "I think I saw a bridge down the road. We'll bring the car across. You'll see our lights as we work our way up toward you."

Hollis recognized Branson's voice.

The lights on the bank disappeared, and a car started up. Hollis had no idea how far away the bridge was that Branson had mentioned. He could hear Soldier still searching close by. The swishing noise indicated that he must have picked up a stick and was poking at bushes.

Hollis remained still and hidden. He wondered if Laura had done the same, or if she had simply kept running. If she had, she would have no way of knowing that she'd be walking into a trap, with two men coming toward her while Soldier closed in from behind.

When the sound of Soldier stomping around and poking trees grew more faint, Hollis pushed to his feet. He stayed close to the river, seeking shelter in the shadows. Anytime it sounded like Soldier was coming toward him, he froze. He kept moving one step at a time.

Off to the side, deeper in the trees, Soldier grew suddenly quiet. A moment later, Hollis heard him say something under his breath. And then Soldier was running.

He must have spotted Laura.

Following the noise of the footsteps, Hollis ran behind Soldier, but off to the side. Soldier increased his pace.

Hollis heard a woman's scream.

And then Soldier grunted. "Gotcha!"

She'd been caught.

Hollis hurried toward the noise, being as quiet as possible while moving as fast as he could. As he drew closer, he heard the sound of a struggle. Laura was putting up a fight. If Soldier could access his gun, he would have used it by now. He must have ditched the rifle or stored it in the car. He would have been slowed in his pursuit of them by having to carry it.

As he approached, Hollis saw movement that was more shadow than substance in the darkness. Soldier must have dropped his flashlight, or it had stopped working. Laura's muffled groans and Soldier's grunts told him that the fight was not over.

Once he was close enough, he saw that Soldier was holding Laura off the ground with an arm around her waist while she kicked at his legs. Then he lowered her so her feet touched the ground and he angled his arm over her head.

Soldier was about to break her neck.

No way was he going to let that happen.

Hollis pulled his gun. Then stopped. Shooting meant he risked hitting Laura. Instead, he lunged toward the struggle. Soldier must have heard him. He let go of Laura and turned just as Hollis raised the butt of his gun to hit Soldier on the back of the head. Instead, he landed a blow to the side of Soldier's head, which only seemed to make him more angry.

Soldier smacked Hollis in the jaw, causing his whole head to vibrate.

"Traitor." Soldier punched Hollis in the stomach.

Though he could not see clearly, Hollis heard a thwack that indicated Laura had picked up something and hit Soldier in the back. Soldier responded with a groan of pain. Hollis pivoted so he could aim the gun butt at the back of Soldier's head.

This time, Hollis hit his mark with a resounding thud. Soldier crumpled to the ground, unconscious.

Laura's hand found his hand in the darkness. "Thanks for coming to my rescue."

She squeezed his fingers. The way her touch made his heart pound had nothing to do with the fight they had just been in. She let go and turned. "We should get out of here."

He grabbed her sleeve. "There are men downriver waiting to ambush us at a bridge. We should be able to spot them before they see us. They have flashlights."

Soldier groaned. It would only be a matter of seconds before he was on his feet again. They had nothing to tie him up with. Hollis struck him again with the butt of the gun hoping that would buy them time.

They rushed into the darkness, preparing to face another possible confrontation and knowing they couldn't backtrack without running into Soldier.

SEVEN

Laura gasped for air. At first, she and Hollis had run as fast as they dared in the darkness over the uneven snowy terrain. Soldier stayed right on their heels.

Once they could no longer hear Soldier behind them, Hollis chose a strategy of moving quietly rather than quickly. He was probably as worn out as she was, if not more. She looked up ahead, not seeing the light that would indicate they were close to the men coming in the opposite direction toward them.

They veered back toward the river. They'd gotten too far away from the road to use it as a reference point. Hopefully, the river followed the road or led somewhere.

"Where do you think they are?" she said.

"I don't know how far away the bridge was that they referenced."

"Maybe we'll just end up slipping past them." That might be too much to hope for.

Hollis didn't say anything, just kept walking. She could see nothing in front of her but the dark outlines of the trees and twinkling stars in the night sky.

After they had walked another ten minutes without seeing or hearing signs of their pursuers, he tugged on her sleeve, indicating that they should sit down.

"I need to take a break," he whispered and then chose a spot on the ground.

"Me, too." She sat beside him.

They were only a few feet from the river's edge. The symphony of water rushing over rocks comforted her in the face of so much danger. She scooted in close to Hollis so their shoulders were touching. Being close to him made her feel safe. "You thirsty?" The water bottle felt really light.

He shook his head. "I need to catch my breath for a moment." He let out a heavy sigh. "Just want to get out of here."

"Wish I knew how close we were to getting to the road that leads into town. Once the sun comes up, it'll be harder for us to hide." The despair she felt clouded her words. She didn't want to give up hope, but it felt like they'd been running forever and not getting anywhere.

He reached over and patted her knee. "I want

to get you out of here so you can say hello to your aloe vera. I'm sure George misses you."

She laughed, appreciating the warmth she heard in his voice and his effort at humor in such a terrible situation. Hollis fell silent. He was probably listening for someone approaching as much as she was.

"That guy, Soldier, almost killed you back there," he said. "That scared me."

She hadn't had time to fully absorb how close to death she'd come. The realization made her shake and then she felt tears slide down her cheeks. Hollis gathered her into his arms. He held her until she stopped crying and then wiped the tears from her face. His touch on her face was like the brush of butterfly wings. Being so close to him felt like the most natural thing in the world.

Even after he pulled away, he kept his arm around her and gave her shoulder a squeeze.

She shook her head. "Until two days ago, my life was pretty boring."

"You never should have been dragged into this."

"I know you tried to stop that from happening," she said. "It hasn't been all bad. You're here with me."

"Yeah, I really know how to show a girl a good time."

"I'm not sorry you came into my life," she said. "My life was a little too boring."

"There arc lcss life-threatening ways to end boredom."

He pulled his arm away. Embarrassed, she wondered if she had been too gushy in expressing her feelings. Despite the bond between them. It felt like Hollis retreated when she expressed affection.

A noise deeper in the trees caused them to fall silent. They were both sitting with their backs to the river on the bank. Laura held her breath as she waited for another sign that Soldier was close. Maybe he, too, had stopped to listen, or the sound could have been an animal.

She dared not move. They had been talking softly, barely above a whisper. If Soldier had been close enough to hear them talking, he would have found them by now.

She stared out into the blackness as tension wound around her chest.

Another cracking noise indicated that someone or something was in the forest close enough for her to hear it.

Hollis had dropped his hand from around her back where he'd been holding her, but now his hand rested on top of hers. Though neither of them spoke, the warmth of his touch calmed her frayed nerves.

Really, she didn't know much about this man who had given away his true character when he'd spoken in such a gentle way and tried to protect her as she'd been surrounded by men bent on violence. But she did know that if it hadn't been for him, she would have been dead by now.

There was another noise in the trees that sounded distinctly human. Laura's muscles grew tight as she let out a sharp breath. Hollis squeezed her hand.

No light came from the forest, which meant that it was Soldier who was moving around as he searched for them without a flashlight. If they tried to run, they risked being caught. The smart strategy was to stay put.

The sound of her heartbeat drumming in her ears amplified as Soldier moved closer toward them.

Stay still, don't move.

There was a thudding footstep maybe ten feet away from where they were and then Soldier grunted. She could see the dark outline of his body above the bush that blocked his view of them.

Soldier turned to face the river.

She held her breath and willed herself into total stillness. He was so close that any noise would give them away.

Shouting came from deeper in the forest. It was probably the other two men approaching. Circles of light through the trees confirmed her theory.

"I'm over here," Soldier shouted. He turned and walked toward the voices.

Hollis turned and started to crawl away. She followed. If the men with flashlights got closer, they would be spotted. They needed to flee.

The voices of the men grew louder. It sounded like Soldier was talking to the other two. She followed Hollis down the riverbank and they sprinted along the rocky shore. The bank would conceal them to a degree, but not if the men came to the river's edge.

As they ran, they heard the men split up. A beam of light panned across the river and they both moved toward the steep bank, pressing their backs into the rocks and dirt. They froze until the light was gone and they heard retreating footsteps.

They moved out again, to the rocky shore by the rushing river, and kept working their way downstream.

They jogged for a few more minutes. Hollis kept glancing off to the side, gazing up the bank.

Lights bounced around.

"They're coming this way," said Hollis.

They hurried up the bank and into the cover of the forest. The light grazed over her arm just as she slipped behind a tree. Heart racing, she kept moving, following the sound of Hollis's footsteps when she couldn't see him clearly.

Without warning, Hollis turned, grabbed Laura and pulled her toward a tree trunk. A light that didn't belong to the river searcher passed by them. The man walked close enough by them that she recognized the stature of Branson as he passed the tree where they were hiding. Branson swung his light, resting it on a tree only feet from where they were.

Laura's heart pounded so hard, she thought it would break her rib cage. She and Hollis were pressed sideways against the tree facing each other, only inches apart. She could feel his breath on her cheek.

After what seemed like hours, Branson pulled the light away and kept walking. Only then was she able to take a breath. Yet they remained there, facing each other and waiting for the coast to be clear.

Finally the noises faded enough that Hollis peered out around the tree. She angled her body to see where the man by the river was. He had moved farther away from them—upriver—and she was grateful for that at least.

Hollis signaled for her to follow him. He

dashed toward a cluster of trees and then stopped to get a bead on their trackers.

For Laura, the noise of the men searching for them had become almost indistinct from the forest sounds. She could only see their lights. She followed the beam and gasped. The man along the river had reversed course and was now coming back toward them.

Before she could alert Hollis, he pulled her against him and whispered in her ear, "Branson is coming back this way."

The two men were closing in on them.

"We need to get out of here."

Hollis grabbed her hand and shot sideways, perpendicular from the river with the men on their trail.

Getting away from the river meant it would be harder to navigate out, but they had no choice. Hollis led her uphill. When she looked down, she could see the two lights and she could make out the bridge with the car parked by it. The metal shone in the moonlight. Unless another man was in the car sitting in the dark, the vehicle was empty. Where had the bald man gone? And they had not seen the second man who had come up in the car. With all that manpower it seemed like they would post someone close to the car. Getting the car though would guarantee their escape. Could they take such a big risk? It might cost them their lives.

A figure burst out of the darkness and knocked Hollis over. Laura had been standing so close to him that she fell back on her behind.

Soldier had found them.

He was on top of Hollis, hitting him in the face.

Frantic, Laura reached for the nearest weapon. She picked up a branch and held it over her head, then advanced on Soldier.

Soldier twisted his body around. "Stay back," he growled as he pulled a knife from his belt.

Laura stopped dead in her tracks. She couldn't help but look down at Hollis. He wasn't moving. Had Soldier managed to knock him out?

Soldier raised the knife and prepared to drive it into Hollis's chest.

Hollis saw the gleam of the knife as it was raised in the air. The blows to his face and head had left him disoriented, but not unconscious. With Soldier's knee pressed into his chest, bracing him in place, he couldn't reach his gun. Yet the potential for death caused adrenaline to surge, so he summoned all his strength and deflected Soldier's hand with a karate chop to the wrist. The knife flew into the grass.

Soldier slapped his face twice and then

jabbed his fist against Hollis's wound. Pain shot through his body. He groaned and arched his back.

"Get off of him." Laura hit Soldier several times with the branch. The weight on his stomach lifted enough for Hollis to wriggle free.

The pain in his shoulder and arm was so intense that he struggled to get to his feet. The only thing that gave him incentive was the fact that now Soldier had gone after Laura. He heard the sound of skin smacking skin and Laura crying out in pain. In the struggle, she must have dropped the branch.

He pushed himself up and staggered to where Soldier was trying to wrestle Laura to the ground. He pulled his gun from the holster and again used it to hit Soldier on the head.

Soldier's response was to whirl around and aim a blow at Hollis's wound again, but Hollis angled out of the path of his fist. Then he used his gun to land a blow to Soldier's face. The man stumbled backward, disoriented.

Laura took advantage of Soldier's moment of weakness and kicked him in the back of the knees. He fell to the ground swaying but remaining on his knees.

If only they had something to tie him up with while they had the upper hand.

Moving slowly, Soldier fell forward and pushed himself up with his hands.

He and Laura ran down the hill. From this vantage point, he could see the bridge and the car, but now there was a light close to the car. Despite the pain still radiating from his wound, Hollis pumped his legs, willing himself to go faster. Laura kept pace with him off to the side.

It took only a few minutes before he heard Soldier lumbering behind them. They had a head start at least. And surely, after taking a couple of blows to the head from the butt of Hollis's weapon, Soldier would be unsteady.

Wasting no time, Hollis worked his way across the hill. Laura stayed close to him as he wove in and out of the trees. When the trees were farther apart, he had a view of the bridge. One of the lights down below had drawn close to the parked car. Clearly, now there was no hope of getting to the vehicle and escaping.

He turned to Laura to tell her the grim news, when far off in the distance way beyond the parked car, he caught sight of twinkling lights. He zeroed in on them. Not enough to indicate a town, but maybe a single home or someone winter camping. "Look—there."

Laura stared out where Hollis had pointed, and a note of hope entered her voice. "We just might make it out of here."

First they had to get to the river, which would lead them to the road and down the mountain. He was fully aware that the men would be looking for them along the road and most likely at the base of the mountain. Though he, too, felt hopeful, he knew they were still not in the clear yet.

The men tracking them had orders that Hollis and Laura were not to get back to civilization alive. He had a feeling they would do everything to make sure they carried out that directive.

EIGHT

As the stars disappeared and the sun rose, Laura was well aware of what easy targets they were. Once they had some light, the location of the mountain road was clear. In order to keep the road in sight, they had to walk where the terrain was flat and open. She had no doubt the men chasing them were equipped with binoculars. There were plenty of high places on the other side of the river where they could perch and watch for her and Hollis. She knew for a fact the robbers had rifles that could shoot at long distances. And because they had the car, they could move up and down the mountain and drop off men at various places to look for them.

Hollis glanced around. "I feel a little exposed, don't you?"

The sun had just begun to peek over the horizon in the east. The sky was still gray. "Just what I was thinking."

Hollis led her toward the brush that grew

close to the riverbank. If they wanted to stay on the move, there weren't many other places to conceal themselves.

They hiked for another hour without encountering anyone. They came to another bridge, this one only wide enough for foot crossings. The bridge, which was constructed of large worn beams placed closely together, was in need of repair. As if its precarious state wasn't enough, Laura feared a man could be hiding behind any of the trees and rocks in the hills on the other side of the river. But she knew they had no other choice. They had to cross the bridge to keep the road in sight.

Hollis stepped across the bridge and turned to watch her cross. Laura was three-quarters of the way over when a gunshot shattered the silence. She dropped to the ground and pulled herself along on her stomach but found crawling over the wooden planks too painful. She rose to a crouch and made a run for it.

Another shot was fired, coming so close to her that her eardrum hurt from the echo of the rifle. Maybe the shooter was closer than they realized. Not stopping, she reached the end of the bridge and Hollis wrapped his arms around her and pulled her down the steep bank. Small stones cascaded around them as they slid down, coming to a stop when their shoes touched the edge of the water.

Hollis pulled her up and led her under the bridge. "I think he was shooting from those hills. If he decides to come after us, it will take him a while to get here. My guess is he'll stay in position and wait for another shot."

Her heart was still pounding, and it felt like her whole body was shaking. Hollis took her hand and led her along the riverbed. They couldn't go back toward the road now—not yet, anyway. They stayed on the move until the sun was directly above them. They stopped and ate the remainder of the food and kept following the river. The creek bed narrowed and grew rockier until they came to a steep drop-off that created a waterfall. It would be too dangerous to try to go down this way.

With the rushing of the waterfall pressing on her ears, Laura peered over the rocks. Down below was a road that ran north and south. The mountain road ran east and west. "Is that that the road that will lead us out?"

Her elation quickly turned to fear when the robbers' car rolled by on the road, going slow enough to indicate that they were searching for Laura and Hollis.

A moment later, a second car went by, going in the other direction but just as slowly. They had recruited someone else to help them.

"How are we going to get out of here?" Laura could hear the desperation in her voice.

"I wonder if they used their phones to call in more men." Hollis pulled out his phone and stared at his screen. "I've got two bars now. We can alert local law enforcement to come out here and arrest these guys and take us in."

"We're miles from town, though. How long will that take for them to get here?"

"It might take an hour or more. I'm calling, anyway." Hollis pressed numbers on his phone.

Down below, one of the cars stopped and two men got out and stared up at where they were. One of the men had a rifle resting on his shoulder.

Laura ducked down behind a rock, pulling Hollis with her. "We've been spotted. I bet they saw the reflection off the phone."

A rifle shot glanced off a rock near her. Hollis crouched closer to Laura. He gave the dispatcher their approximate position and described the cars the men were driving.

She lifted her head above the rock. The man with the rifle had taken a position on top of the car. The other was working his way up toward them, but at a diagonal angle. He must have been assuming they would work their way down toward the road. Plus, it was too steep to climb directly up.

Fully aware that the man with the rifle would take a shot if they became visible, Laura chose a path away from the country road, meaning they had to backtrack.

Hollis put his phone away and crawled over the rocky terrain behind her. Two more shots were fired at them before they got to the softer ground and were able to move faster, back toward the trees.

As they both jogged, Hollis leaned close and said, "Let's move parallel to the country road as much as possible."

She took in a breath between words. "I. Agree. It's the. Only. Way. To. Get. Out. Of here."

Her body was already so fatigued that she just wanted to lie down and rest. As they drew closer to a cluster of trees, she willed herself to keep moving. It felt like she and Hollis were in a labyrinth that they couldn't escape from. And worse, around every turn, danger lurked.

No matter what, she wasn't going to give up. Hollis strained forward, his lips drawn into a tight line. She wondered if he was praying and if it would help at all. She prayed, too.

God, if You are there and if You are real, get us out of here alive.

Praying eased some of the tension in her body. When they got to the cluster of trees, they slowed down. Hollis turned his head and offered her a smile. He reached out and squeezed her arm. "We've come this far. We can make it."

The prayer she'd said still echoed through her mind. "I hope you're right."

They walked as far as they could through the trees until they had no choice but to be out in the open again. When she looked back, she saw a man in the distance coming up over the steep incline. And he was headed right toward them.

Hollis burst into a sprint when he saw the man come up over the rise and make a beeline for them. It was hard to tell from this distance, but the man didn't have the build of Soldier or Joe, or the blond hair of Branson. He was one of the new recruits. From this distance, it looked like he was holding a handgun. He wouldn't be able to get off an accurate shot unless he got closer. Not that that seemed to be a problem. The way the man was closing in on them indicated that he was not exhausted, like he and Laura were.

Though tired and hurting, Hollis took Laura's hand as they tried to maintain distance from the gunman. He was mindful of remembering where the road was even as they moved in such an erratic pattern.

The man dogged them for miles as they worked their way up and down hills. The country road down below came into view and then disappeared. Around late afternoon, the terrain flattened out, and they could see the road most of the time, though they were at least half a mile from it.

A truck went by on the road. The Christmas wreath on the front grill made him think it didn't belong to the robbers. They'd been driving a dark sedan and silver SUV. He watched the truck as it slowed down and made a turn onto a dirt road in the trees on the opposite side of the road.

"There must be a house down there...or something," said Laura.

The man chasing them was still about a quarter mile behind them. This part of the landscape was flat and open. The pursuer would be able to see where they'd gone. That meant that if they followed the truck, they would be putting other people's lives at risk .

As if she knew what he was thinking, Laura said, "We have no choice, Hollis." She glanced back at the gunman closing in on them.

Hollis weighed the options. It might be that the robbers wouldn't want to risk more violence and being caught by involving other people. There was no way to predict that. On the other hand, once he and Laura got to the road, they might encounter one of the cars. The man following them could be communicating their position via cell phone.

The possibility of finding help and ending this nightmare decided for him. Laura was right. Following that truck was their only choice.

He glanced over his shoulder. The gunman was still closing in on them, but he had not yet stopped to make a phone call. Maybe he had decided he could take them out on his own.

Hollis led Laura to the road and across to the other side. It was a few hundred yards to where the truck had veered off into the trees. They both sprinted away from the main road and into the trees, toward where the turnoff was.

They came to the dirt road and hurried down it. Both of them slowed to catch their breath. After a couple of turns up and down the road, they still saw nothing but forest. Time was running out. Once the pursuer on foot phoned the men in the cars, Hollis had to assume that it would be a matter of minutes before the cars turned onto this road.

Without any sign of the truck or a building of any kind, Hollis began to doubt his decision. What if the house was miles from the main road?

Hollis looked over his shoulder. "We shouldn't be so out in the open, huh?"

They moved off the road and into the forest.

The sound of a car behind them made them sprint even faster. Through the trees, he could see one of the searchers' cars drive by. They slipped deeper into the forest, making sure they were out of sight. Several minutes later, the car rolled back through, still moving slowly. Both Hollis and Laura had taken shelter behind a tree.

That was a good sign. The cars must have found out where the truck had gone, not seen them and just turned around. It also meant that wherever the truck had gone must be fairly close.

They trod lightly over the deadfall, constantly glancing toward the road. Up ahead, he could see a truck through the trees. As they drew closer, the Christmas wreath on the front indicated it was the same truck they'd seen earlier. Both of them ran to the clearing, where the truck was parked by a river. There was a firepit and a picnic table, both covered in a layer of snow. No house. And the driver of the truck was nowhere in sight.

Hollis was fully aware that the criminals' cars could come back this way once they made it out to the main road and still hadn't found them. "The guy in the truck must be here somewhere."

Laura ran toward the truck and looked inside, and then in the empty truck bed. "Why do you suppose he came out here?"

Hollis peered through the forest, where he thought he saw movement and color through some brush. "I think he's over there."

It took a few minutes to get to where he'd pointed. Hollis saw a tall man in a Santa hat. The man was bent over sawing at the base of a small evergreen.

Hollis feared they would frighten him if he just spoke up. The man finished sawing the tree. He must have sensed that someone was behind them and turned to face them. His initial reaction was shock. It was clear on his face.

After two days of being on the run, Hollis was sure he and Laura must have looked like something the cat dragged in.

Laura stepped forward. "Sir, we don't mean to frighten you, but we're in a pretty precarious situation."

The man's expression softened.

"It's a long story, but if we could just get a ride into town," said Hollis.

"I saw you on the news." The older man pointed at Laura. "You're that lady who was kidnapped by those bank robbers."

Hollis breathed a sigh of relief that they would not have to go into a deep explanation of what had happened to them. They needed to get out of here.

"I'm glad you know who I am." Laura reached

out for Hollis's hand. "This man helped me escape."

"Sure, I can take you both back into town." The older man lifted up the tree. "For my grandkids to decorate."

The man seemed like a genuinely good person and Hollis hated the idea of putting him at any risk. There was still the chance of encountering the robbers once they got to the main road. They might be waiting there and decide it was worth hurting this man to get at Hollis and Laura. "Is there a back way for us to get into town? I'm concerned that the men who are after us might find us if we go the way we came."

The man in the red hat thought for a moment. "We can do that. This road is a giant loop that comes out at a different place on the main road."

"That works for us," said Hollis.

Within minutes they were sitting in the warm cab of the man's truck, with Laura in the middle and Hollis in the passenger seat. The truck wound through the forest and then came out to the main road.

After about twenty minutes of driving, Laura rested her head on Hollis's shoulder and fell asleep. He was glad she felt safe enough to do that. There had been moments when they were on the run that she had expressed affection for him. Her ability to hold herself together under such strain amazed him. She had a quiet, sweet quality that he was drawn to, but she had made it clear that she had little faith in prayer or God, something that mattered a great deal to him.

Hollis stared at the road up ahead. He wasn't sure where he and Laura stood. His focus needed to be on this investigation.

He knew that the men would not give up so easily. They would come after him for revenge and after her because they feared she could identify the man on the tablet screen. The man who had planned the robberies. If the mastermind behind the robberies wanted them dead, he was sure the order would be carried out with tenacity. He couldn't let his guard down just yet.

NINE

Laura woke up to the sound of Hollis and the other man sharing fishing stories as the truck rumbled down the road. In the distance, she could see the outskirts of the town of Clark River, where the robbery of the First Federal Bank had happened. She hadn't known that Hollis liked to fish. Though she had probably shared the most harrowing experience she'd ever had with him, she knew very little about the man she sat next to. What she did know was that he was brave.

"Hey, sleepyhead." Hollis turned to look at her. Affection coated his words. She saw a deep warmth in his eyes that made her heart flutter.

"Sorry, guess I was really out of it." They had clearly bonded over what they'd been through and now they would probably part ways. That must be why all this intense emotion was coming up.

What was going to happen once they got back

into town? Would they go their separate ways? She imagined the police and the FBI would want to question her. Why was she even wondering if she would not see Hollis anymore?

"Where should I drop you folks off at?"

She looked at Hollis. "I know I probably need to talk to the police, right?"

Hollis nodded with a nervous glance at the older man. He probably didn't want to discuss too many details about the case. "Yes, that needs to happen."

"Can I go back to my hotel first? I really need a shower and a bite to eat."

"I don't know if that would be safe. It's a small town. I'm sure it wouldn't be hard for those guys to find out where you were staying."

"Please, all my stuff is there." A note of desperation had entered her voice. She realized that she was still shaken by all that had happened. Not being able to get her personal things felt like the final blow.

"Okay, only if I stay with you. I'll need some time to make some calls, anyway," said Hollis.

She was grateful for more time with Hollis.

The older man slowed down once he was inside the city limits. "Where are you staying?"

"The Western Inn," said Laura.

"I know where that is." The older man stopped at one of the town's three lights and hit his blinker.

He pulled into the parking lot of the hotel. She looked around for her car, then realized it was still at the bank parking lot, where she'd left it the morning of the robbery. They both got out, thanking him and saying goodbye. When Hollis offered the man money for his trouble, the older man waved him off. "You two just take care of yourselves."

Her hotel key was still in her purse at the bank, so they went into the office, where a teenager with purple hair greeted them from behind the desk. She instantly recognized Laura. "You're back. I saw you on the news. Your boss has been calling here wondering if we'd heard anything. The police came by, too."

Hollis stood behind her. "She's been through a lot. We'll take care of things. Could you just give us a new key card for her room?"

"Are you with the police?" The young woman with purple hair fixed her gaze on his torn and dirty clothes. "Are you the one who found her?"

"You could say that," Hollis said. "The key card, please."

The teen turned toward the wall that contained little cubbies and pulled out a key card. Laura was grateful for Hollis's assertive nature. She was not in the mood to relive the last two days.

They crossed the courtyard to her room. "The

bank is walking distance from here. I would assume my purse and car keys are still there. You don't have a car?"

"It's forty miles from here, so it wouldn't be linked to this crime if it was found. We all traveled in the van to Clark River from the hideout."

She used the key card and pushed the door open. It felt like she was looking at someone else's stuff—the open suitcase on the luggage rack, packed in her efficient way, the neat stack of books by the bed. She stepped inside and realized she was not the person who had left this room two days ago, the one who liked the predictability of computers and the safety of schedules and order. After what she had been through, she was a very different person. For one thing, she was stronger than she'd realized. She had faced death more than once.

She pulled a change of clothes from the suitcase. "I won't take long."

"Do you have a phone charger? My phone is almost dead. I need to call my boss and see what we need to set up for you to try to get an ID on the man you saw on the screen."

"So it's the FBI I'll be talking to?"

"The robbery case is federal. But the local police will help with other charges and catching these men since they're probably still in the area. We both can ID the other three robbers."

A chill ran up her spine. "Reason enough for them not to want us to get to the police, right?"

His expression grew very solemn. "Neither of us is safe yet. They may come after us again."

His words echoed in her head as she stepped into the bathroom. She showered and changed, then ran a comb through her hair. When she came out, Hollis was pacing the floor and watching the parking lot through the window.

"You can shower, too, if you want. I think we would still have time to get to the bank before it closes."

"I don't have a change of clothes." He touched the five-o'clock shadow on his jaw. "I'll just splash some water on my face and clean up as best I can." He drew the curtains closed. "You might want to take a chair away from the window."

Did Hollis think the robbers might try to shoot her through the window? Hollis had already expressed concern about that. If she'd been all over the news, the possibility of being found here was even greater.

Hollis came back out looking cleaner and like he had combed his hair. "I should have enough battery power on my phone to call the local police to give us some protection. How far away is the bank from here?"

"Just two blocks. If I had realized it was that

close when I went to work there, I would have left my car at the hotel."

Hollis phoned the police and let them know the situation and who he was. "We'll come in and make a statement, but we need to stop at First Federal and get a meal before we come over there to file a report. Some protection would be nice." He listened to the response on the other end of the line. "Okay." He addressed his question to Laura. "Where did you want to eat?"

"There was a restaurant at the other end of town that was recommended to me."

Hollis explained where they would be going and then hung up. "I need to leave my phone here to fully charge it."

"That's fine."

They stepped outside into the chill of late afternoon. Snow was lightly falling. Her winter coat was still at the bank. Once again, she was grateful for Hollis's warm coat.

As they walked the short distance to the bank, she found herself staring at every car that drove by on the street or was parked. When they arrived at the bank, a police car was already present.

The officer got out and shook hands with both of them. "I'm Officer Waddel. I was there the day of the robbery. So glad you made it back okay."

She thanked him. "I'll just go inside and get my purse and phone."

"I plan on following you to the restaurant," said Officer Waddel. "And then we can make sure you make it to the police station safely."

As she was walking toward the entrance, she heard Hollis describing the cars they'd seen the robbers driving. He must have forgotten to do that when he made the initial call.

Laura peered through the glass doors of the bank and saw Angela behind the counter. At twenty minutes before closing, she was probably the only teller there. Laura swung the door open and stepped inside. When Angela saw Laura, she ran to give her a hug.

"The police called and said you were okay. I was so worried about you. What a horrible ordeal." Angela squeezed Laura tight. The older woman's eyes were damp when she pulled free of the embrace.

Tears rolled down Laura's cheeks as well. "Probably the most frightening thing that I have ever been through."

Angela shook her head for a moment. She patted Laura's arm. "Did they catch the men that did this terrible thing?"

Laura turned back to where Hollis was talking to the officer in the parking lot. "Not yet. We still have to makc our statements to the police."

"We?"

"Long story," Laura said. "I assume my purse is still here?"

"Oh, yes, of course. I locked it up." Angela made her way back behind the counter. She bent over, disappearing from view. When she popped her head back up, she held the purse.

Laura stepped toward her, reaching for the purse.

The next few seconds went by in a blur. She heard gunfire. The windows that faced the street shattered. There was more gunfire and then a car sped away. Somewhere in that time, Laura had dropped to the carpet on her stomach.

Angela screamed. "Behind the counter! Get behind the counter with me!"

Laura could see her purse three feet away, where Angela must have dropped it. She left it there and crawled toward the counter.

When she looked over her shoulder and out the glass doors to the parking lot, she could not see Hollis or the officer.

More gunfire erupted. But this time it wasn't a spray of bullets, like what had come from the passing car, but one shot after another, as if from a rifle.

She reached the counter and slipped behind it next to Angela. Angela wrapped her arms around Laura.

Before she could take a breath, the squeal of tires alerted her to the car returning. The windows that looked out on the drive-through shattered. Shards of glass flew through the air. Both women screamed and crawled to get out of the way of the sharp projectiles. She remembered that smaller banks like this often couldn't afford bulletproof glass.

Outside, the car engine revved and tires squealed and then it fell quiet.

Laura didn't trust the silence. She was shaking and her hand was bleeding from where she must have touched broken glass. The two women crouched behind the counter holding each other for at least a minute.

When she pulled away her first thought was of Hollis. The possibility of anything bad happening to him caused a wave of nausea. She pressed her hand on her stomach and closed her eyes. The fear paralyzed her.

Had the police been called? There hadn't been many people around when they'd walked to the bank, but maybe someone had phoned for help.

Angela gasped for breath as she spoke. "There's a silent alarm."

Laura turned her head to where Angela had indicated under the counter. Of course, the police would come if they weren't already on their way. She pushed the button. That must have been the alarm that had been disabled the day of the robbery.

"Do you think they'll come back?" Angela asked.

Laura could only shake her head. Shock was setting in and she was having a hard time comprehending what she should do next. She feared she would hyperventilate.

They both remained behind the counter sitting on the floor. The numbness was wearing off, because she felt pain. She stared down at her hand, where she felt the sting of the glass cut.

"Laura, Laura." Hollis's voice was filled with anguish.

She burst to her feet and ran into his arms.

"Thank God you're okay." He held her tight.

"Just a little scuffed up. I was so afraid one of those bullets had hit you."

She relished the safety of his arms but knew that the robbers had shown they would come after them again one way or another.

Sirens blared down the street as Hollis hugged Laura. He had lived through five terrifying minutes of thinking that she'd been killed.

He turned to face the parking lot, where two police cars had just pulled in, but still held Laura in a sideways hug. She seemed very shaken. Her knees buckled and he steadied her.

When the first round of gunfire had occurred, he and Officer Waddel had taken shelter under the patrol car, which had protected them when the car came back a second time. The patrol car, though, had been shot to pieces.

Two of the arriving officers were working their way up and down the street, directing much of their attention toward a building where Hollis was pretty sure a sniper had been. This was a small town, so they didn't have a SWAT team and the police probably had limited rapid-response training. The five officers who had shown up were probably the entire police force. Another reason why the rural banks were more vulnerable.

The bank teller who had been present at the robbery came up beside them and they all stepped outside, where an EMT guided the teller to the ambulance that had pulled up.

Laura lifted her hand to show Hollis she was bleeding. Still holding her, they walked to the ambulance.

"This woman needs medical attention," said Hollis.

The EMT ushered Laura up two metal stairs and through the open doors of the ambulance, where Angela was already seated.

Officer Waddel approached Hollis.

"Did you catch the sniper?" Hollis was sure the shooter had taken aim from the roof.

Officer Waddel shook his head. "We think he may have been picked up by a different vehicle at the back of the building."

The men must have gotten into town and been watching the hotel and maybe the bank, waiting for the first moment when he and Laura were most vulnerable. The plan had been executed efficiently and quickly. "Look, I know that our description will help you guys, but I need to get Laura out of here and to a safer place. These guys might come back for round two."

Office Waddel nodded. "I get that, but they also might leave the area. The sooner we have descriptions, the sooner we can put out alerts to neighboring counties."

"I can't afford to lose Laura as a witness. That has to be my priority. Soon as we get her to a secure place, one of our guys can sit down with us and put together a sketch of the other men."

Waddel straightened his spine, indicating that he wasn't crazy about the idea. He pulled a notepad out of his back pocket. "Why don't you give me basic descriptions of each of the three men? We have the vehicle descriptions. Maybe that will be enough to get us started."

Hollis described the build, hair color and unique features of each of the men. Soldier had some tattoos on his arms and neck that might make him easier to identify. The other men would blend in pretty easily.

He was fine with the locals bringing in these guys. The Bureau would have an opportunity to question them down the line. It was the big fish that Hollis was after, and Laura was the only one who had seen him so far, even if it had only been on a tablet screen.

Laura came out of the ambulance with a bandage on her hand.

Hollis turned toward Officer Waddel. "Could we have some protection back to the hotel and maybe someone could at least follow us to the county line?"

"Let me go talk to my supervisor. I know city police and the sheriff's office are going to want all hands on deck to catch these guys before they fall off the face of the earth." Waddel walked a few yards to where another officer was leaning into his car talking on the radio. The other officers who had arrived on the scene had already dispersed.

Laura came and stood beside Hollis. "What's going on?"

"It's not safe for us to stay here in this town. I'm going to try to arrange for a deeper level of protection for you."

She drew the open ends of the coat he had

loaned her closer to her body. "I assume we can go back to the hotel room so I can get my stuff?"

"Sure, I need to get my phone, anyway."

"I suppose that's the way it has to be. I don't know why I thought I would be back to work at my job in the next few days."

Laura looked so shaken and forlorn already, he didn't want to break it to her that her life might not go back to business as usual for a very long time. "Good thing George the aloe vera can take care of himself. Hope you don't have to miss Christmas with family."

She managed a smile. "I don't have any family close by. I usually just have dinner with a single coworker who's in the same situation."

For some reason, that kind of a Christmas struck Hollis as sad. Most of his family had moved to other states, but he had an aunt and uncle who lived in Montana.

Officer Waddel strode back over to them. "I can escort you back to the hotel and I'll follow you to the county line. But if I get a call that the men have been located, I'm going to have to respond to it."

"Understood." Hollis cupped the other lawman's shoulder. "I appreciate it."

Hollis walked with Laura back into the bank to get her coat and her purse with the car keys and phone. Her expression changed when they stepped inside the building—glass was strewn all over the place. He rested his palm on the middle of her back, hoping that would help steady the emotions that must have been raging inside her. "Don't think about what happened. We just need to pick up your things."

Hollis imagined that crime-scene people would be coming from a larger town.

Laura nodded. "I can do this."

She stepped carefully around the broken glass and reached down to pick up the purse. A waterfall of glass particles fell off it.

Once she grabbed her coat, they stepped outside. "I'm still very hungry," she said.

"Me, too. We'll figure out something, but I need to make some calls to arrange where to take you."

She opened her purse and pulled out car keys. "You can drive. I really don't think I have the focus right now."

They walked the short distance to her car and got in. It had been parked on the other side of the bank, out of the line of fire. Officer Waddel, in one of the other patrol cars, was right behind them as Hollis pulled onto the street and headed back to the hotel.

They weren't safe staying here in Clark River. But given the nature of the attack and how quickly it had been planned and cleanly executed, one question rang through his head. Were they safe anywhere?

TEN

As they pulled into the hotel parking lot, Laura's stomach growled. She was pretty wrecked by all that had happened. Trying to function on an empty stomach would only make things worse. "I know you need to make calls right away. But I need something to hold me over until we can get some real food. I think there's a vending machine in the office."

Hollis parked the car right by the door to her hotel room. "Have Officer Waddel escort you."

"Do you want something?"

"Yeah, I'm pretty famished," Hollis said.

The police officer pulled in right beside them. She handed Hollis the key card and got out of her car. The sky was turning gray, and she realized it must be near dinnertime. Her stomach growled again, reminding her how little she'd eaten in the last two days.

Officer Waddel had already gotten out of his patrol car.

"Can you go with me over to get snacks?" She pointed toward the office.

He nodded.

Hollis glanced up and down the street before slicing the key card through the slot and disappearing inside.

While she was in the lobby, Officer Waddel waited for her outside. His stance—shoulders back, feet apart, hand close to his gun—suggested a level of high alert. Laura selected peanut-butter crackers and granola bars, the healthiest options from what she could see. Thinking that some quick energy food might be good, too, she pushed the button for two candy bars. Hopefully, they would be able to eat some real food soon.

Officer Waddel fell in beside her as she made her way across the parking lot and knocked on the door to her room. Hollis opened it right away and waved her in. He held his phone close to his mouth.

She opened the curtains a few inches so she could see Officer Waddel outside still watching the street and pacing a short path back and forth in front of the hotel room.

She opened the package of peanut-butter crackers and handed them to Hollis. Hollis took them, giving her a slight nod as a thank-you gesture. He put one in his mouth while he listened on the phone.

The voice on the other end of the line was not on speaker and came through as muffled. Hollis gave one-word answers and then grabbed a piece of hotel stationery that he must have found earlier. He picked up a pen and wrote something down.

Laura finished her snack, which didn't do much to curb her hunger. She ate the candy bar and then set the second one down by the crackers Hollis hadn't finished yet.

She grabbed her toiletries from the bathroom and tossed them in her already packed suitcase. After retrieving her charger, she zipped the suitcase shut. She picked it up, preparing to take it outside.

Through the narrow gap in the curtains, she saw Officer Waddel jump in his car and zoom out of the parking lot. He must have seen something. A moment later, another police car rushed by with its sirens flashing.

The action caught Hollis's eye, too. He pulled the phone away from his face. "Stay in here. Get away from the window."

Her hearted pounded as she left the suitcase by the door and retreated to the chair that was out of view of the window. Hollis drew the curtains fully and stepped back as well. He finished his phone call and told her the plan.

"There's a field office seventy miles from here. They have the setup for us to work on you ID'ing the man you saw on the tablet, as well as finding a match in the criminal database for the three men I did the robbery with."

"What about Officer Waddel? He must have seen one of the cars. That's why he left," said Laura.

"We can't wait for one of the officers to escort us. Time is of the essence here." He picked up her suitcase. "I'll take this out and move the car, so the passenger-side door is facing the hotel. Two steps and you'll be in the car."

She nodded. She pulled her phone from her purse. "Text me when it's okay for me to come out." Standing by the window and watching would be too dangerous. "What's your number?"

He recited his number while she entered it into her contacts and then she did the same for him.

Hollis opened the door and disappeared. The room was nearly dark with the curtains drawn and only one bedside lamp turned on. It was so quiet she heard the hum of her car engine as Hollis moved it.

Her phone dinged.

Good to go.

Feeling intense trepidation, she rose from the chair. It would be nothing for them to come by and spray her car with bullets like they'd done at the bank.

She got to the door and twisted the knob. Hollis had left the key card on the dresser for the maid to find. The door would lock behind her. She swung it open. It was only a few steps to get to the car.

Hollis waved at her from the driver's seat as she hurried and grabbed the passenger-side door. Hollis pulled forward even before she had clicked into her seat belt. He zoomed across the parking lot and out onto the street.

As he drove toward the edge of town, a car got in behind them but turned off on a side street. She glanced up each street that connected with Main Street, thinking she would see flashing police lights. They passed one other car going in the opposite direction before they reached the edge of town and Hollis sped up.

She closed her eyes and took in a breath.

When they had driven less than a mile, Hollis checked his rearview mirror. "Hey, look who made it."

Laura turned her head to see the patrol car behind them. The tension coiling through her limbs and stomach subsided. "I wonder if the police tracked down any of those men who shot up the bank."

"Officer Waddel's number is in my phone." He pointed toward the console, where he had placed his phone.

She picked up the phone just as it rang. The name above the number said Waddel.

"Hello, Officer. This is Laura."

"It's not me in the car." Officer Waddel sounded panicked.

"What are you talking about?"

"He stole my car and tied me up. Another officer just found me."

"What is he saying?" Hollis must have picked up on the level of terror raging through her.

"One of the robbers stole the patrol car."

A sudden impact on the rear bumper caused the car to fishtail. Laura gripped the armrest and swallowed the scream that threatened to escape.

Clenching his teeth, Hollis gripped the wheel as the car snaked down the two-lane highway, crossing the double yellow lines several times. At least there was no oncoming traffic.

Once he had the car under control, Hollis pressed the accelerator. As the needle shot past eighty, he was glad the roads weren't icy. The patrol car remained close for miles. Hollis glanced at the green road sign that indicated how close they were to the next town. Ten miles and they would be able to pull off. For sure, he couldn't take Laura directly to the field office. Even if the man in the patrol car didn't manage to run them off the road, Hollis didn't want him knowing where they were going.

"He's getting really close again," Laura said.

Could they make it for ten miles?

"I'm turning off into that little town up ahead to try to ditch this guy."

Hollis pressed the gas pedal all the way to the floor when the highway straightened out. He put a little distance between himself and the patrol car.

A voice came through on his phone that Laura still held in her hand.

"I never hung up," she said. She drew the phone closer to her face. "Hello… Yes… Okay. We're going to pull off at Jewel." She pressed the off button and then looked at Hollis. "The police have another car coming this way to try to catch this guy. And they've alerted the highway patrol."

Eventually, the road had a number of curves, so Hollis slowed a bit and focused on his driving. The stolen patrol car slowed as well, allowing Hollis to maintain their distance.

He pulled away even more once the road

straightened out again. Billboards advertising restaurants, hotels and a chance to dig for Montana sapphires lined the highway.

He was grateful when the exit sign popped up. A mile later, he took the only exit for Jewel. The patrol car followed them onto the exit ramp.

The town sign said the population was two thousand people. At breakneck speed, Hollis turned off on the first side street that he saw. He wove through a neighborhood that had older small homes, most of them with twinkling lights and inflated Christmas characters on the lawn. The edge of town came up quickly as they rolled past a trailer court. He found a cutoff that looked out on an open field. He drove into the field, spinning the car around so he had a view of any vehicle coming from the two streets that intersected with the field.

"Do we just wait?" Laura asked.

"I'm hoping he searches for us on Main Street and assumes we pulled back out onto the highway. Did you notice if he was close enough to see where we pulled off when we got into town?"

She shook her head. "If he did, he might just attempt another drive-by, like he did at the bank."

The fear he heard in her voice was not unexpected. "I think our best option is to wait this out. I don't want to lead them straight to the

FBI field office." He glanced over at the trailer court, where there didn't seem to be much activity. "Can you hand me my phone?"

Laura gave him the phone and he called Officer Waddel to let him know where they had last seen the stolen patrol car.

Laura stared through the windshield as well. That her nerves were raw was evident by the way she bit her lower lip.

His stomach growled. Neither of them had had anything but the snacks that Laura had gotten from the vending machine. He touched his stomach.

"I actually heard that," she said.

"I promise we'll get some food the first chance we get."

They waited for another five minutes, both of them tense and focused on watching the area around them. Neither spoke.

Thinking they had eluded the stolen cop car, he finally started the car and rolled forward. He wove through the side streets until he had no option but to go back to Main Street in order to return to the highway. They came to the edge of town. When he checked the rearview mirror, he saw that a patrol car was parked at the gas station across the street from them. He couldn't see who the driver was from this distance. It could have been the police car that had come looking for the one that had been stolen.

The car didn't pull out and follow them.

When he got back on the highway, it was dark. His headlights cut a wide swath in front of him as the dotted yellow line clicked by.

Laura pointed through the window. "There was a sign for a truck stop five miles up ahead. We can get something to eat there."

"Okay." Maybe they had something they could grab quickly. Sitting in a restaurant would leave them too vulnerable.

When he checked his rearview mirror, there were headlights behind him. Hollis said a prayer that the car behind him was just someone who needed to go somewhere, not a robber who wanted to run them off the road.

ELEVEN

The car behind them remained close but never surged forward or tried to pass them. Laura had gone so long without substantial food that she was getting a headache. The lights of the truck stop glowed up ahead.

Hollis turned off and parked by the restaurant. Only one other car was there, but at least seven semitrucks were parked some distance from the restaurant at the edges of the large lot.

She assumed the car that had been behind them had sped by.

She pushed open the door. The cool night air surrounded her as she got out of her car. "I'm starving."

Hollis joined her on the sidewalk and held the door for her. Several of the tables were occupied by men eating alone, as were two stools at the counter. The truckers, she assumed. A family sat at one of the booths—a mom and dad with two girls under the age of five.

The waitress looked up from the silverware she'd been wrapping in napkins. "Have a seat anywhere, honey. We're not busy right now."

Hollis stepped closer to the counter. "We're in a bit of a hurry. Do you have a quick meal to go?"

"I could put together two fried-chicken dinners for you. Comes with mashed potatoes and green beans."

Hollis glanced over at Laura to see if she was okay with that. Right now, she would eat just about anything. "That sounds perfect."

"All righty then," said the waitress. She disappeared behind the swinging doors that led to the kitchen.

Laura stepped closer to Hollis when she saw another car pull up outside. Though the car was not a police vehicle, the driver remained behind the wheel. She reached out for Hollis's hand and then tilted her head toward where the car had just pulled in. She noticed it was parked away from the streetlamps so she couldn't see what the driver looked like.

Hollis had been smart to get a meal to go. It wasn't safe for them to be out in the open for too long.

The waitress returned with two to-go containers. Hollis paid for the meals, and they headed outside. When they got outside, the driver of the other car still had not gotten out. It wasn't a car she recognized as belonging to the robbers. Not that they couldn't have acquired another vehicle.

Hollis handed her the to-go boxes and got behind the wheel. As they pulled out of the huge parking lot and headed back toward the road, she glanced over her shoulder. The other car was no longer parked by the restaurant.

Hollis rolled onto the two-lane road and sped up. "I think we can find a turnout here fairly quickly so we can eat."

He'd only driven for five minutes before he slowed down to park at a lookout point surrounded by trees. He parked the car so he had a view of the road in both directions, then he turned off the engine and the headlights. Someone speeding by would not notice them.

"Sorry, kind of dark," said Hollis. He clicked on the flashlight on his phone. "Not exactly a candlelight dinner but we can at least see to eat."

She wondered why he was thinking about candlelight dinners. The image of looking across a table at Hollis while the flames of a candle danced, being drawn in by his subtle smile and gentle voice, warmed her to the marrow. Maybe someday.

She handed him one of the to-go containers. When she opened her Styrofoam box, the scent of the chicken greeted her nose. She tore open the package of plastic utensils. The chicken was still warm, as were the mashed potatoes. They both ate without talking. The breading on the chicken had the most perfect spices.

When he'd eaten the last bite of green beans, Hollis wiped his mouth with the paper napkin. "Man, that hit the spot."

She took the last few bites of her potatoes. "Just wonderful. Here, give me your container."

He handed her the empty to-go box, which she set in the back seat.

He started the engine and turned on the lights. "We've got a long drive ahead of us. At least it's nice to be doing it on a full belly."

He pulled out on the road. For miles, there were no cars behind them or passing them going the other way.

Hollis found a radio station that played soft instrumental Christmas music. Laura fell into a restless sleep, waking periodically to see the yellow lines click by and to gaze at the stars in the sky. Then she fell into a deeper sleep. When she woke up, they were on a highway where there were only a few other cars.

"How close are we?"

"Less than ten miles. Can you grab my phone? In contacts, there should be a number for Luke."

She picked up his phone off the console and clicked through to his contacts. She noticed several women's names as she scrolled down to find Luke. "You know lots of people."

"I have a big extended family."

She had seen only a narrow part of Hollis's world. He had a life outside of his work as an FBI agent. He might even have a girlfriend. The notion made her sad. Candlelight dinners or not, she had no claim on him and that made her even sadder.

"Luke is the agent who is going to help us ID the men. I know you're tired. I am, too, but this can't wait. I need you to text Luke and let him know we're ten miles out."

She sent the text. As they drew nearer to town, behind her she noticed headlights that remained close to her car. When Hollis took the exit into the town, the car followed them.

Hollis drove past hotels and gas stations and through a residential part of town. She was relieved to see the car did not follow them. He parked in front of a two-story office building, where only lights in one first-floor window glowed.

A car rolled by on the street and turned the corner up ahead. Laura tensed up. She could not live like this long-term, being on edge all the time.

Hollis must have sensed her trepidation. "You're pretty safe in a field office with two trained agents."

Hollis pushed the car door open.

Laura clutched her purse and opened her door. Hollis escorted her to the office. The door swung open and a tall man with gray hair greeted them.

"You made it." Luke stepped to one side to allow them to come in.

Hollis let Laura go in first. She noticed that Hollis did a quick survey of the street before going inside.

"I've got everything set up in the office." Luke led them down a hallway into a room. The space consisted of two desks, one with a laptop and the other with a desktop computer. Luke pointed to the office chair and looked at Laura. "Have a seat." He walked across the room to retrieve another chair.

Hollis explained the setup to her. "Luke has access to the national criminal database. Most of the low-level guys in the robberies have records. We should be able to identify the three men I was working with pretty easily. If my undercover assignment had lasted longer, I would have been able to do that in the field."

Luke indicated that Hollis should sit in the chair he'd scooted across the floor. Then he told him, "I think the most efficient thing to do would be to have you look through the database and punch in the information that you gleaned about the three men and their descriptions. I'll work with Laura using the sketching software to try to put together a picture of the man she saw. I've already got the program open for you, Hollis."

Luke sat in front of the laptop and Laura pushed her office chair toward the screen. Hollis clicked away at the keys and watched the monitor.

Luke opened up a program on his laptop and proceeded to ask Laura about the facial features of the man she'd seen. He questioned her about the shape of the eyes and how far apart they were, changing those features at her suggestions and then moving on to the shape of the head, hairstyle, nose and mouth.

As the features were added, the face didn't look right to her. "I'm afraid of making something up to fill in a blank because I can't remember."

"We'll do the best we can," Luke said. "When the face looks right, you'll know."

She did remember that a lid of one of the man's eyes was droopy.

After about an hour of work, Hollis shared what he had figured out. He had found out the real name of the man known as Soldier largely because of his neck tattoo and his extensive criminal record. Because Joe had let slip that his hometown was not far from where the botched robbery had taken place, Hollis was able to find out who he was as well. Branson remained a mystery.

Hollis stood up to stretch. "I'll get the information I have sent over to the Clark River Police Department so they can work on catching Joe and Soldier. Bringing those two guys in won't stop the robberies, though. We still have to get the head honcho."

Luke clicked a few more keys on his laptop and then angled the screen so Laura could look at it.

"It's close, I guess." She shook her head. "The thing that this drawing can't capture was the way the man held his head and the intensity of his gaze. If I saw this man again, I would recognize him."

"I can see you're really tired. Maybe after a few hours' rest we can go back to this. There's a cot and blanket in the next room if you want to sleep."

"I could use a nap," Laura said. She looked at Hollis, who was still typing on the keyboard. "After you have a good picture of the man I saw, I can go back to my old boring life, can't I?"

Luke glanced at Hollis.

"Maybe with a little extra protection just to

make sure they're not going to keep coming after you." Hollis didn't sound too sure of himself.

"I assumed he wanted to kill me to prevent me from giving you his description. Now that you have it, do you think they'd come after me purely for revenge?"

Hollis pushed away from the desk and turned to face her. "You still might need to testify in court once he's caught."

Feeling the weight of what she faced, Laura placed her palm on her chest and shook her head. She still had a target on her back.

"Right now, you're the only one who has seen the man behind these robberies." Hollis rolled his chair closer to her so he could touch her arm. "I know this is a lot to deal with. Why don't you get some sleep? I'll talk to my supervisor as soon as he's in his office to see what we can do," Hollis said.

Laura found the little room with the cot. There was also an easy chair, a table with magazines, snacks and a coffee maker. Agents must use it when they were pulling an all-nighter, she mused. A sleep machine sat on the floor by the cot, already plugged in. Laura lay down on the cot and pulled the blanket up around her shoulders.

She could hear Luke and Hollis talking in the next room. Her name was mentioned. Were they discussing her fate? She reached down and turned on the white-noise machine and tried not to think about how long she would be under protection and looking over her shoulder.

After he sent the information about Soldier and Joe to the Clark River police, and Luke stepped out to patrol the area, Hollis collapsed in a chair in the reception area of the field office. He nodded off.

Sometime later, he wasn't sure how long, he thought a noise outside had awakened him, though it might have been part of a dream. He saw movement outside. Someone walking through the parking lot. Hollis burst to his feet and checked the computer room. Luke had not yet returned.

Laura was fast asleep in the break room.

After grabbing his gun, Hollis returned to the reception area. Luke had locked the door as a precaution. Hollis unlocked it and stepped outside.

He heard the sound of two men in a struggle, grunting and flesh slapping against flesh. He turned on the flashlight on his phone and shone it toward where the noises had come from. Luke was holding Joe in an armlock.

"Look who I caught sneaking around."

"Arrest me. I don't care anymore. I'm tired of this." Joe's voice was filled with anguish.

"How did you find us?" Hollis stepped toward the two men.

"We guessed you were FBI and would go to a field office. Men were sent to watch the two closest ones to Clark River," Joe said. "Once I saw her car, I called it in. More guys are on the way over here."

Luke said, "I'll take care of him, and try to get some more firepower here. Maybe we can take in some more of these guys. You need to get Laura out of here to a safe place."

Hollis turned to go back to the office. Hauling Joe, Luke was at his heels. Once inside, Hollis stepped into the room where Laura was. He shook her shoulder then leaned down to turn off the sleep machine.

Laura stirred.

"We need to get out of here."

"What…why?"

"No time. Let's go." He lifted the blanket off her.

Laura sat up but it was clear she was not fully awake. She swung her feet around to the floor. "What happened?" She rubbed her forehead.

He reached down to take her hand. "I'll explain on the way. We need to go."

He led her out of the back room to the reception area. She took a step back when she saw Joe handcuffed to the chair he sat in.

Luke was on his phone to local police trying to get more law enforcement over to the office. He waved at them as they passed through.

They stepped out into the dark parking lot and to Laura's car. Another car was pulling into the lot—a police car. It could be Luke's help, or it could be the robber who had stolen the police car. They weren't going to stick around to find out.

Hollis got behind the wheel and sped through the lot just as another car pulled in. He prayed that Luke would be okay.

Laura snapped her seat belt and looked at him. "So now can you tell me what happened? I'm gathering they found us, but you guys caught Joe?"

"Yes, he told us there were more men on the way to the field office."

"Then by now they must know that the FBI has all the information I could give them."

"Not quite. That sketch was helpful, but you said yourself you think if you saw the guy again, you'd recognize him."

"Yes, if I heard him speak and saw the way he carried himself. The guy just had a very domineering demeanor, even on a screen."

Hollis was checking the mirrors to make sure

they weren't being followed when a thought occurred to him. "We think the banks were cased for some time before the robberies. I wonder if our guy appears on any of that bank footage."

"I was hired by First Federal to shore up their security systems. The alarms and the cameras were not working when I fired up the computer just as the bank opened. That means the robbers knew the layout of the place before they entered it. They knew where the silent alarm was."

Hollis wanted to ask Laura more detailed questions about her work. She might still be a help in the investigation. Even though they had no footage of the actual robberies, he wondered if there might be something of significance in the days leading up to each robbery. Other agents had gone over the footage, but maybe she would see something they hadn't. It was a needle-in-a-haystack situation—hours and hours of tape to watch from before the various robberies, so they would need to know what to look for.

But for now, the first priority was getting her somewhere safe.

He shot her a glance. "Can you take my phone and find Aunt Gin in the contacts?"

"Yes, but why?" she asked as she picked up his phone.

"I'm taking you to a bed-and-breakfast that she runs. We'll be safe there temporarily."

Laura scrolled through the screen. "I found her. What do you want me to say?"

"Tell her that I and a friend need a place to stay and that we'll be arriving late. No need for her to get up."

Laura typed in the message.

He took an exit ramp that led to a country road. Though traffic was light at this hour, there had been cars behind them. The test to see if they were being followed would be if another car turned off after them. This road led only to country homes and farms. He saw no headlights behind him as he navigated the exit.

"Where is this place we're going to?"

"The Silver Forest Inn. My aunt and uncle have run it for years. They have cross-country skiing in the winter and hiking in the summer."

He turned down another narrow road.

"You don't think they'll find us here? They found us at the field office. How hard would it be to figure out you have relatives in the area?"

"They figured out I was an FBI agent, which would have been easy enough. All bank robberies fall under the jurisdiction of the Bureau. But the other robbers only knew me by a fake first name."

Laura's concern was not unfounded. The mastermind might have a way to find out his real name. "I think we'll be okay at least overnight as long as we are not followed. This place is pretty hidden."

The road wound deep into the mountains. As he approached the inn, he saw streetlamps that illuminated the parking area and then the Christmas lights Aunt Gin had strung around the porch. Hollis and his siblings had spent almost every Christmas and part of the summer here. The house itself looked like it had been transplanted from a Bavarian village.

"It's like something out of a fairy tale." Laura's voice was filled with wonder. "It looks so peaceful here."

Hollis had been coming here all his life. He supposed someone seeing it for the first time might get that impression.

"The door will be unlocked. We can just go inside." There was only one car in the parking lot, which meant there was one guest. His aunt and uncle parked behind the inn.

They got out and headed toward the wraparound porch. Hollis pushed open the door and they stepped inside the great room, which featured a rock fireplace and three sitting areas. A huge Christmas tree done in shades of blue and silver dominated the room, and miniature lights twinkled everywhere.

"It's really beautiful," said Laura.

"Aunt Gin goes all out for Christmas. Lots of decorations and food and family."

"Wow, it sounds like something out of a movie."

He caught the note of sadness in her voice. "Everybody's Christmas looks different. The important thing is that the birth of Jesus is celebrated."

"I guess. It was always just me and my dad, and it really wasn't that big a deal."

He wasn't sure how to respond to that. He could not picture a life without family and big celebrations. "That room off to the side has its own bathroom. If the door is open, the room is vacant. I suspect Aunt Gin put her only guest in one of the upstairs rooms. I'll go get your suitcase and leave it outside the door for you."

"Thank you." She headed down the hallway.

Hollis went outside and pulled Laura's suitcase from the back seat. Laura's concern that the robbers might find them had to be considered. But even with all the resources the man behind the robberies seemed to have, it might take some time to connect Hollis to Aunt Gin and Uncle Dave. He hoped, anyway.

They'd have time to at least get a good night's sleep. All the same, he chose to sleep on a couch facing the front window. If anyone did pull up to the place, he would be ready for them.

TWELVE

Laura awoke to the smells of bacon and coffee. She put on her robe and wandered toward the enticing aromas. The sound of laughter greeted her even before she entered the kitchen. She walked through a dining room with a huge table that sat twenty people and into the kitchen where there was a breakfast nook with a smaller table.

Hollis was sitting at the table with an older man who had hair that resembled cotton balls. Both men were sipping coffee. Hollis's hair was wet from showering and he had a fresh set of clothes on that were a little oversized on his lean frame. A woman with her back to the door stood in front of a huge griddle frying bacon and flipping pancakes.

"Morning," said Hollis. "Laura, this is my Aunt Gin and her guest, Travis."

The man with the white hair nodded in her direction.

Aunt Gin turned around and smiled. "Good morning. Welcome to the Silver Forest Inn. Breakfast will be up shortly."

Hollis's aunt had candy-apple-red hair and bright green eyes.

Hollis stood up and pulled out a chair for her. "Have a seat. Can I get you some coffee?"

"Sure," said Laura.

"Uncle Dave is outside with my cousin Charlie. I'm sure they'll be in for breakfast."

Laura took a seat.

Travis leaned close to her. "I'm their best customer. I come up here to do some sketching and painting and enjoy the outdoors."

"Travis is more family than a customer," said Aunt Gin as she piled bacon and pancakes onto serving plates.

"I work off some of my bill by helping out with the upkeep. Used to be a contractor," said Travis.

Just as Aunt Gin put the plates of food on the table, including a breakfast casserole she'd had in the warmer, the door swung open and an older man and a man who could pass for Hollis's brother came in.

Hollis poured Laura a cup of coffee and introduced her to his uncle and cousin. The scents of the bacon and pancakes wafted up to Laura's nose while everyone bowed their heads and said grace. Out of respect for her hosts, Laura bowed her head as well.

There was a time when she had believed in God and talked to Him all the time. The disillusionment had come as a teenager. But she had called out to God when she and Hollis were on the mountain and she feared she would die. Maybe deep down, the faith of her childhood was still there just buried under disappointment and pain.

After the prayer, everyone lifted their heads.

"Let's dig in," said Charlie.

Plates were passed around and conversation jumped from one subject to another. She loved hearing Travis's stories of wildlife encounters while he hiked, and Charlie and his father talked about the repairs they needed to get done. Hollis and Charlie shared memories of the times they had at the inn when they were younger. She found herself feeling relaxed and delighted as she ate her breakfast. This was what it was like to have lots of family around. As a child, she had dreamed of something like this.

As the meal was concluding, Hollis leaned over and whispered in her ear. "I've made some calls. We need to leave as soon as possible."

She nodded, his comment a reminder that the meal had only been a brief oasis from the ongoing threat they were dealing with. Hollis probably didn't want to bring trouble to his aunt and uncle's door, either. The longer they stayed here, the more they put everyone in danger.

Charlie and Uncle Dave tossed their napkins on the table and excused themselves. Travis and Aunt Gin started to gather up dishes. Laura moved to help them.

"No, dear," said Aunt Gin. "You run along and get ready to go. Hollis explained to me the urgency of what you two are working on even if he didn't give me the details."

Laura's spirits lifted. Hollis saw her as a partner who was helping him with his case. She offered him a smile that she hoped communicated gratitude.

"I'll just shower and get dressed." She returned to her room and got ready quickly. When she stepped out into the great room, Hollis was reading a newspaper and waiting for her. She was sure he would explain what he had in mind once they were alone in the car.

Aunt Gin emerged from the kitchen with two lunch boxes. "A little something for the road."

They walked to the door.

Aunt Gin took Laura into a warm embrace. "You are a precious thing."

Laura thought she might cry. How she had longed to hear those words from a mom when she was younger.

"We need to get moving," Hollis said. "Thanks for everything." He hugged his aunt.

As they made their way to the car, Aunt Gin stood on the porch and waved. "Safe travels."

They got into the car and Hollis shifted into Reverse while Aunt Gin remained on the porch watching them.

"Your aunt hugged me like I was her long lost relative," Laura said.

"She's like that. My whole family are a bunch of huggers."

"You've been given a beautiful gift, Hollis."

"It's yours for the taking," said Hollis. "They'll welcome you in anytime. You saw how they were with Travis."

As they pulled out of the driveway, Laura pondered what he had said. Happy family gatherings were something she thought only happened in television shows. It also meant she would see Hollis in the future. Being with him felt so right. Though she doubted the feelings were mutual. He seemed to be all about his job, and she held a piece of information that might help him find the man behind the robberies.

Hollis turned onto the road that led out to the highway.

Right now, she couldn't picture a future when she wouldn't be on high alert and waiting for another attack. She glanced over at him. He smiled back at her as heat rose up in her cheeks.

"What?"

"I was just… Thank you for the offer of sharing your family with me," she said. "I might have to take you up on it."

He was still grinning as he stared out at the road ahead. There had been a little spark of attraction between them.

"So why don't you tell me what your phone calls were about?"

"I've arranged for us to have access to the bank footage that was taken the days before each of the robberies. What we're thinking is that the guy who planned the robberies may actually have scouted the banks prior to the heists. Maybe if you saw him on camera, we could get a clear ID."

It still seemed that his main reason for having her with him was that she could help his investigation. All the same, she could not deny the power of the moment that had passed between them. "That must be a lot of footage."

"Yeah and it's not edge-of-your-seat viewing. We'll start with the day before each robbery," Hollis explained. "We'll be going to a different field office this time. And I've arranged for a secure place for you to stay at night."

Where the country road met the on ramp to

the highway, she noticed a battered old blue truck that looked like it had been abandoned pulled off the road.

Hollis turned onto the highway and traffic increased.

The robbers knew what her car looked like and they may have followed them right up until Hollis turned onto the road that led to the inn. "Do you think maybe we should get a different car?"

"Probably."

His eyes flicked to the rearview, then back to the road. "We've got a bit of a drive. I'm taking you to the field office in Bozeman. It's about two hours away."

Laura held up the containers with the meals Aunt Gin had so lovingly prepared. "At least we won't go hungry."

"You never go hungry when you're around Aunt Gin."

As they sped along the highway, Laura noticed the battered blue truck she'd seen by the on ramp was behind them.

"Are you looking at that old truck?" Hollis glanced in his rearview mirror again. "I noticed it, too."

"It was parked by the on ramp. I just assumed someone had abandoned it."

"He's stayed behind us the whole time."

They couldn't be sure the truck was following them. But after everything that had happened, they needed to remain alert.

Hollis found a classical music station on the radio, but kept the music turned down so they could talk when needed. Both of them kept eyes on the blue truck, which never passed them, and only changed lanes from time to time.

As they approached the exit, she watched as the blue truck got in their lane and followed them into town. Once they were downtown, she lost sight of it. Hollis wove through an industrial park to a three-story commercial building.

"Get all your stuff that you need out of here. I'll arrange for your car to be parked somewhere safe but not out in the open."

"Should we even be here? They found the other field office easily enough."

"We need access to the robbery tapes. This office has the setup for that. This work might help us close the case and catch the man behind the robberies," Hollis said. "What I can do is get some more agents here as well as alert the city police. Like I said, we have a secure place to take you at night."

"I suppose they would be reluctant to come after us with all that firepower around us. How long will it take to look through all the footage?"

"The FBI got access to all the footage from all the robberies for a week before the heists occurred. We could get a warrant for even more. We'll work until you're tired, if that's okay."

She didn't answer right away. It was important to end the robberies, and if she could help with that, she had a duty to do so.

He reached over and put his hand on top of hers. "I know you're scared. I want to assure you I have taken every precaution to make sure you're safe."

She met his gaze. "I know you have, Hollis. And I'll help you as much as I can." She stared out the window. She liked that he didn't pull his hand away. The warmth of his touch calmed her frazzled nerves. "Realistically, I can't go back to my old life until this guy is caught, anyway."

"I think that's a fair assessment," said Hollis.

She nodded, letting that reality sink in. "Let's do this, then."

As they unloaded her suitcase, purse and the lunches Aunt Gin had prepared, she found herself surveying the streets that surrounded the office building. Her stomach clenched.

Hollis took her suitcase, and she gave a backward glance to the parking lot before they stepped inside the FBI office. Except for the dated earth-tone carpet, it looked very similar to the other field office. They stood in a reception area, which had a desk, couches, a coffee machine and a water cooler. Behind the desk was a long hallway.

Hollis put down the suitcase and looked down the hallway. "Agent Phillips was supposed to meet us here."

Laura's heart beat a little faster. No way could the robbers have gotten here before them. Could they?

What if the blue truck had just followed them long enough to see which city they were going to? Joe had said they had staked out the two closest field offices. Maybe they still had a man watching this one.

"Is this office the second closest to Clark River?"

"No, the one in Helena is closer." Hollis headed down the hallway. "Maybe Agent Phillips is still setting stuff up."

Laura waited. She could see the parking lot through the reception-area windows. She stepped out of view and set down her purse and the lunches.

She jumped when the outside door swung open. A woman dressed in a dark suit and holding a cardboard tray with three coffees stood just inside the door.

"I'm Agent Marisa Phillips. You must be Laura. Where's Hollis?"

Laura let out a breath. "Down the hall looking for you."

Agent Phillips set the coffees on the desk. "I thought you two might need some fuel. You've got a long day ahead of you. This stuff is way better than what I brew with the coffee maker. Lots more caffeine, too." She reached for one of the cardboard cups and handed it to Laura.

"Thank you." The cup warmed her hands.

Hollis emerged from the hallway and greeted Agent Phillips with a hug. "I was a little worried about you."

"Just stepped out to get you some coffee," Marisa said. "Why don't you two get to work? Let me know if I can help with anything. The files are all downloaded, dated and ready for you to look at."

Hollis told Marisa about the suspicious blue truck and then asked if she would get another agent over here, as well as inform the city police of the threat level. He handed Laura's car keys to her. "If you could make arrangements for that car to be stored out of sight and get us another vehicle, we'd appreciate it."

"Your wish is my command." She grabbed another coffee and handed it to Hollis.

They headed down the hallway to an office where there were several chairs and a wraparound desk with keyboards and monitors.

Hollis set down his coffee after taking several sips. He pulled out one of the chairs, sat down and wheeled toward a keyboard. "We'll start with the very first robbery." He typed and then looked up at the monitor. "This is going to be a little less exciting than watching paint dry, so I'll put the tape on double time. We can slow it down if you see anything that you want to look at more closely."

Laura took a seat as well.

Hollis clicked a few more keys and the screen showed the interior of a bank lobby. Two employees entered after unlocking the front door.

They watched footage from all the banks, drank their coffee and ate lunch. She studied the screens intently, until the point that her eyes felt like they had been smeared with Vaseline. Several times, Hollis left the room. She could hear him talking to Marisa in the hall.

The banks were all owned by different entities. They all probably had slightly different security protocols and systems. The only way someone could rob them would be to have intimate knowledge of the bank.

Hollis came back in the room.

She turned to look at him. "At what point were the panic button and the cameras disabled?"

"When we interviewed the tellers, their memories were often unclear because of the trauma, but it seems it happened first thing and fast. That's why there are three to four men on each robbery. With the robbery I was on, it was Joe's job to do that."

"So the robbers would have had to know exactly where the panic button and the main switch for the cameras were. No time to fish around." She drew her attention back to the screen.

Hollis sat down beside her and pushed the play button. "Right. In two of the robberies, the cameras were shot out."

She moved her attention back to the footage and watched for another twenty minutes.

Her eyes caught on a man on screen. "Stop the tape."

Hollis sat up straighter in his chair, feeling his heart flutter. Maybe all the hours they had invested would pay off. "Tell me how far to rewind."

Laura leaned closer to the screen as the tape backtracked. "Right there."

He stopped the tape. She stood up and pointed at a man wearing a baseball cap. "There. That man. He's aware of where the cameras are." She studied the screen intently. "I've seen him before on one of the other tapes. Only he had on a cowboy hat."

"Let's watch for a few minutes and see what he does."

The man appeared to be wearing a workman's uniform. He moved in and out of the frame. At one point, he carried a toolbox.

"He must have been hired to fix something." Hollis scooted his chair closer to Laura's so he could see better. "Any guesses where you might have seen him before?"

"I've watched a lot of footage. Let's start with the second robbery, the bank that had all the plants."

It took a few more hours before they found the man in the cowboy hat. He did have a similar posture, gait and build to the man in the baseball hat. The man always made sure never to look directly at the camera. This time, he was watering plants.

"We can have a tech go through the footage and see if there is ever a time when he messes up and we get a face shot of him. That would be too time-consuming for us."

Hollis stared at the still image of the tall man in the cowboy hat. "So he must get into the bank for several days as a workman of some sort or another."

"That would allow him to watch the employees, see their habits and get an understanding of the security systems," Laura said.

Hollis pushed back his chair. "This is good stuff, Laura. It's progress. It's been a long day. How about we call it? I'll take you to the safe house. You can get dinner and get some rest."

"Are you staying with me?"

He was flattered that she trusted him so much and wanted to be with him. "Yes, and we'll have an officer parked outside the house as well."

"Well, I'm tired of looking at a computer screen. I wish I could go for a walk or at least run on a treadmill to clear my head."

He laughed. "I don't know if the safe house has exercise equipment, but maybe you can run up and down the stairs."

It took only a few minutes for them to gather up their things. Agent Phillips was waiting for them in the reception area. She tossed Hollis a set of keys. "Your chariot awaits."

Hollis caught the keys. "Thanks. Were you able to line up some extra protection?"

"The one agent who's close enough would have had to be pulled off of an assignment. The city police have agreed to patrol the safe house several times during the night." Agent Phillips grabbed her coat from the back of a chair. "I'll follow you out to the safe house."

"Sounds good." Hollis grabbed Laura's suitcase.

When the three of them stepped outside to the parking lot, it was dark.

Marisa pointed at a white sedan. "That's your new ride over there."

Hollis headed toward the car, then looked down at his key. There was a button that indicated that the vehicle had a remote starter. He pressed it.

All at the same time, an ear-splitting boom sounded, Laura screamed and debris flew through the air. The car he'd been about to get into exploded in front of him.

THIRTEEN

The blast from the explosion lifted Laura up and slammed her on the ground. She landed on her behind. Her ears were ringing as bits of metal and glass showered down on her.

Agent Phillips's face appeared in front of her. The other woman cupped Laura's shoulders with her hands. Marisa mouthed words but Laura shook her head, unable to hear anything. The explosion must have caused temporary deafness.

As Marisa stood up and pulled out her phone, Laura scanned the area for Hollis. She saw him lying on the concrete on his back, not moving. Hollis had been the closest to the explosion.

Still too stunned and weak to get to her feet, she crawled toward the motionless Hollis feeling like she'd been shaken like a rag doll in a dog's mouth.

As she drew near to him, she saw that blood dripped from his forehead. She reached out to touch him just as lights flashed in her peripheral vision. A minute later a paramedic kneeled beside her. Another paramedic ushered her away to an ambulance before she could see if Hollis was breathing.

The paramedic guided her inside the ambulance and motioned for her to sit down. The bright lights made her wince.

The idea that Hollis might be dead caused her to take in a ragged breath. Her entire body tensed.

The paramedic was a young man with a buzz cut and high cheekbones. When he got down on her level to look her in the eye, he, too, spoke words she could not hear. She guessed he was asking her if she was okay.

She shook her head.

While the paramedic took her vitals, another ambulance showed up. Several paramedics surrounded Hollis. She watched as he was put on a stretcher. It felt like someone had stabbed a hole in her stomach. Was Hollis going to be okay? Was he even alive?

The paramedic examining her hung up the blood-pressure band and pointed at her hands. For the first time, she looked at her palms, where tiny pebbles were embedded in the skin and blood oozed from several scrapes. She hadn't even felt any pain.

She was barely aware of the paramedic doctoring the wounds on her hands. All her attention was on the ambulance that was taking Hollis away, its sirens blaring. Her stomach clenched. He must be seriously injured.

An EMT poked his head in the door and said something to the paramedic that she couldn't quite discern. She still couldn't hear anything but a whooshing noise in her head. The experience gave her a sensation of floating.

The EMT disappeared.

The paramedic got Laura's attention by squeezing her arm just above the elbow.

He mouthed the words. She read lips well enough to guess that he was saying something about taking her to the hospital.

She nodded. She was probably going to be okay, once her hearing came back, but she really wanted to find out about Hollis. The paramedic indicated that Laura should lie down.

Snow was swirling in the air as the paramedic closed the doors and the ambulance started rolling. The EMT must have gotten in the driver's seat and taken off.

When they arrived at the hospital, Agent Phillips met the ambulance. She stared down at Laura as she was wheeled in on the gurney.

"How is Hollis?" She could hear her own voice, but it sounded hollow.

"They're still checking him out." Agent Phillips's voice sounded far away, but at least Laura's hearing was coming back. She squeezed Laura's hand. "I'll let you know as soon as I know something."

Laura was taken to an exam room, where she waited for a doctor. While she was alone, she had time to piece together what had happened. The robbers had to have been watching the parking lot for some time to have seen her car there and known that they were inside. The bomb had been triggered by the remote starter. She shivered. If Hollis had waited until they were in the car, they both would be dead now. But how had the robbers known the new car was the one that Hollis and she would be using?

The doctor came in and her thoughts halted. He was a redheaded man who looked too young to be practicing medicine. After he checked her pupils and her vitals, he asked, "When you were blown back by the blast, how did you fall? Did you hit your head at all?"

His voice sounded normal.

She looked at her bandaged hands. "I think my hands took the brunt of the landing."

After thoroughly examining her eyes and ears, the doctor asked her a few more questions, told her that she was free to go and left the room. Laura wandered out into the hallway, where she found Agent Phillips sitting in a waiting-room chair.

Laura sat down on the couch beside Marisa. "Any word on Hollis?"

Agent Phillips shook her head. "Not yet. They released you, I assume?"

"Yes, I'm fine. Just some bruises and scrapes," said Laura. "I don't get it. How did they know to plant the bomb in that new car?"

Agent Phillips wiggled in her seat and ran her hands through her hair. "My best guess is that they were watching the office for some time. They must have seen me drive away in your car and come back in that other car."

Laura shuddered and clutched her collar at the neck. "I hope Hollis is going to be okay."

"Me, too. Not only is he a good agent. He's truly a decent human being."

"Yes…true." Laura thought about what Marisa said. Hollis was more than that to her. The thought that he might be dead had made her realize that she cared deeply about him.

Marisa rose to her feet. "Look, I'm going to go hunt down some hot tea or cocoa while we wait. Do you want some?"

"That would be nice. Thanks."

Laura watched a woman at the nurses' station type on a keyboard. There was no one else in the hallway. She stared at the festive Christmas decorations that hung from the ceiling and the lighted garland around an office door. All of it created a sense of warmth and welcoming that Laura was having a hard time engaging with. The world felt too chaotic right now, so filled with uncertainty. Was it even possible to have the peace and joy that Christmas carols referenced?

Marisa returned with two steaming paper cups. "Nothing like cocoa for comfort food, huh?"

The two women sat and waited. Laura had just finished her last sip of cocoa when a doctor emerged from a side hallway and walked toward them. The expression on his face gave away nothing.

The doctor addressed his comment to Marisa, who must have talked to him previously. "He wants to be released. He has some cuts and bruises from the explosion. He had a previous wound where a bullet grazed his pectoral muscle and shoulder. We patched that up a little better. He lost consciousness, which means he probably has a grade-three concussion. He needs rest, both physical and mental."

Laura took in a deep breath. Hollis was going to be okay.

"We can make sure he gets that," said Marisa.

"Good. Then the nurse will bring him out shortly." The doctor turned on his heel and left.

Laura wasn't sure why Marisa had used the word *we*. "What's going to happen now?"

"I'll take you both to the safe house, as planned, and I'll stay there with you to help with Hollis and provide a degree of protection. What happens in the morning is up to Hollis. This is his case."

A moment later, a nurse wheeled Hollis down the hallway. Her breath hitched when she saw him. His face was gaunt, as though he'd been drained of energy.

She rushed toward him.

Hollis rose from the wheelchair.

Though she wanted to hug him, she patted his upper arm. "I'm so glad you are okay."

"Don't know why they make me sit in one of those things." He pointed back toward the wheelchair. He smiled at Laura. She leaned a little closer to him.

"I'm ready to go. Marisa, I assume you can take us to the safe house?" he said.

"Plus, I'll be staying the night. You're in no condition to be on duty alone."

"I'm not going to argue with you about that," Hollis said.

"Great. I'm in the side parking lot."

As the three of them walked together through

the hospital and outside, Laura was keenly aware that they could have been followed to the hospital. One of thc robbers might be waiting for them outside.

They stepped outside into the cold winter night. Hollis knew how vulnerable they were. There was only one hospital in this town. The robbers could have been watching for the explosion to happen and known he and Laura had been taken there.

Hollis directed his question to Marisa. "Did you arrange for a search of the area after the car blew up?"

"My focus was on you and Laura. Sorry, I dropped the ball."

They were about twenty feet from Marisa's car. "Give me a second to check for explosive devices," said Marisa. She pointed at Hollis. "You stay put."

Though he still felt very weak and he wasn't going to argue with Marisa, Hollis did not like being sidelined.

While Marisa checked under the car and searched inside the doors and under the dashboard, Hollis surveyed the parking lot as the falling snow twirled in the lights. "We can't let our guard down."

Marisa waved them toward her. "All clear."

Laura reached for the back door and got in while Marisa climbed behind the wheel. Once he was seated in the passenger seat, Hollis remained vigilant about his surroundings. As Marisa pulled out of the lot onto the dark street, he watched his side mirror to see if any other car followed, or at least pulled out of a parking space. This late at night the lot was not full. It would be easy enough to see a car turn on its lights and head their way.

"All clear?" Marisa kept her eyes on the road.

"I think we're good, but you might not want to drive directly to the safe house. I'll keep watching." Hollis still felt weak from all that his body had endured. He saw spots in front of his eyes, and he had a headache.

"Gotcha," said Marisa. "I won't take a direct route."

Hollis looked over his shoulder at Laura. "You okay?"

She folded her arms over her chest and nodded. She was probably as battle weary as he was.

"That was a lot to handle," he said.

She brushed a stray hair off her face. "I'm pretty worn out."

He found himself wishing that he could hold her and let her know it was going to be okay. But the truth was neither of them was safe, not anywhere.

Marisa drove through neighborhoods where the yards glowed with Christmas decorations. She took a detour past the downtown shops, which all had darkened windows.

"This part of town doesn't have any traffic at night. It'll be easy enough to see if we're being followed."

She turned onto a side street and came to stop by a house that had no lights on.

"Let's put your car in the garage in case they troll the streets looking for it," he said.

Marisa tossed him the house keys. "Get Laura safe inside first."

When Hollis opened the back door, he reached a hand out for her. She looked up at him. Beneath the streetlamp, he could see that her eyes were filled with trust and warmth. He led her to the door and unlocked it. He took note of the cars that were parked on the street.

Once inside, he flipped on a light and stepped into the garage to open the door for Agent Phillips.

When he returned to the living room, Laura had turned on a single lamp by the couch. She stood only a few feet away from him, gazing at him pensively. As if she was waiting for instructions.

He took in the layout of the place. The living room and kitchen were visible from where he stood. The stairs probably led up to the bed-rooms.

"If you want, you can go upstairs and get settled in. I have to talk with Marisa for a few minutes to make sure we're on the same page security-wise."

She nodded, turned slightly and then pivoted and fell into his arms. He held her close for a long moment while she let out a single sob.

"I don't blame you for reaching your break-ing point." He stroked her hair with his hand, relishing how wonderful it felt to have her in his arms. Grateful that she had sought comfort from him.

After a long moment, she pulled away. Still in his embrace, she gazed up at him. "I just want this to be over," she said.

He could get lost in the warmth of her gaze. "Me, too."

As he looked into her eyes, he found himself wishing her could kiss her. Time seemed to stop. His fingers trailed down her cheek. If only they could stay in this moment.

Laura spoke first, breaking the intensity of the moment. "What happens tomorrow?"

"Not sure. I'd like to go over the interviews we did of the bank employees who were pres-ent at the time of the robberies."

"I'm going to try to get some sleep." With a

backward glance at him, she trudged toward the stairs.

A second later, Agent Phillips emerged from the garage. Hollis knew it hadn't taken that long to pull the car in and close the garage door. He guessed that she'd seen Hollis hugging Laura and had waited politely.

Marisa stepped into the room and pulled her gun from the shoulder holster. "Since you're not a hundred-percent physically, I'll take watch downstairs. If you want to come down and spell me in four or five hours, that would be great. But I think you really should get some rest. What's the plan for the investigation moving forward?"

He shook his head. "We need a break in the case. If we can get some kind of ID on the guy that Laura saw in two of the banks leading up to the robbery, that would help. What we think is that our mastermind finds a way to case each bank, usually by having to do some kind of work inside."

They talked a few more minutes, then Marisa reached out and rubbed his arm. "Get some sleep, Hollis. You look really worn out."

He couldn't argue with her. He already had a headache, which might be connected to the concussion. A deep sense of despair sunk in as he walked up the stairs. The door to the first room was closed. That must be where Laura was sleeping. The memory of holding her in his arms lifted his spirits. Though he knew he had to let go of the idea that there could be anything between them as long as her faith was in a different place than his.

He chose a bedroom that faced the street and looked out the window for any suspicious activity.

Satisfied that there was nothing to be alarmed about, he got into bed. His thoughts went around in circles as he tried to figure out how he could keep Laura out of harm's way and move this case in the right direction. He prayed, asking God for help and guidance.

As he drifted off, no solutions came to him. It was just a matter of time before the thugs came after them again. He feared that next time they would be successful in killing Laura and him.

FOURTEEN

Laura awoke in total darkness. She was lying on her back, eyes open but unable to make out the details in the room. She'd fallen asleep fairly quickly but kept waking up. Her dreams had been about the footage she and Hollis had watched. Her unconscious mind was trying to figure something out.

She remembered a lamp being on a nightstand by the bed. She reached out, fumbling around until she found the switch. The small bit of illumination was enough for her to get around the unfamiliar room. She rose from the bed, still trying to figure why she was so stirred up. She couldn't stop thinking of the layout of each of the banks she'd viewed. She could only guess at the security setups.

Laura stood at the window. Her room faced the backyard. Beyond the fence were silhouettes of other houses.

As she gazed out at the quiet, dark neighborhood, the thought that she had been wrestling with began to crystallize. Hollis understood investigations and playing a part as an undercover agent, but she understood security systems. If she could go to the banks that had been robbed, maybe even get permission to look at the security setups, would something about the mastermind behind the robberies become evident? Did any of the bank employees remember him when he had been casing their bank?

She did not want to face the idea of being kept in some sort of protective custody until the man was caught and tried. She wanted to get back to her work. Over and over, the mastermind had managed to find her and Hollis. The only thing that would stop him would be prison bars.

She looked out the window again. This time there was light moving toward the backyard of the safe house. Her breath caught.

The light disappeared down a side street. She doubted it was just be an insomniac out for a walk or someone taking their dog out.

The light appeared again, still moving toward the fence that surrounded the backyard. Heart pounding, Laura hurried into the hallway. "Hollis, someone is coming this way." She reached for the switch that lit up the hallway.

Hollis came to the door of one of the other rooms. Despite his quick response, it was clear from the way he swayed and blinked at the bright lights that he had been awakened from a dead sleep.

Agent Phillips called up the stairs. "What is it?"

Hollis rushed down the hallway past Laura. "Intruder. Turn on all the lights downstairs—maybe that will scare him off."

Hollis disappeared down the stairs. Laura came to the top of the stairs so she could hear what was going on. The area flooded with light.

"I see him." Marisa yelled. "He's headed back over the fence. I'm going to see if I can catch him. You watch Laura."

Laura heard a door slam. A moment later, Hollis appeared at the bottom of the stairs. "Take shelter in your room. I'll stay in the house to make sure he doesn't try to breach it through a different door."

Laura returned to her room. She crouched low against the wall, bringing her knees up to her chest. After several minutes had passed, she raised herself up to the window. The whole neighborhood was dark except for two bobbing lights that drew close to each other and then drew apart. An intense sound cracked the silence. Someone had fired a gun. Seconds later, lights in the neighboring houses went on.

Laura wanted to run downstairs and find out

what was going on, but she knew she needed to wait until Hollis came for her, just in case it wasn't safe. She had no idea who had fired the shot. Or if Agent Phillips was okay.

Pressing her back against the wall, she stared at the ceiling. She found herself praying once again.

That Marisa would be safe. That she and Hollis would not be under assault.

A moment later, she heard the sound of sirens and footsteps coming up the stairs. Hollis appeared in her doorway. "We need to go. Marisa will stay here and explain things to the police."

"What happened?"

"I'll explain on the way. Let's go."

A hundred questions raged through her head as Hollis reached out his hand for her and led her downstairs to the garage. The answers would have to come later.

Marisa met them at the bottom of the stairs and gave Laura a quick hug. "They know where the safe house is. It's just a matter of time before they come back."

Though she was grateful to see that Marisa had not been shot and for the quick explanation she had given, she still worried about the agent's safety.

Hollis pulled her toward the garage. She got into the passenger seat. Marisa stood on the threshold and pressed the garage door panel while Hollis got behind the wheel and backed out.

The garage door closed almost immediately as they sped down the street. She could see the flashing police lights down the block.

Laura pressed her palm against her chest, where she could feel her heart pounding.

Hollis's gaze seemed to go everywhere at once. "Agent Phillips took a shot at the guy who was approaching the house and scared him away, but there might be others around here. They were able to find the safe house. I doubt they just sent one guy to take us out."

Her breath caught in her throat. Hollis was probably right about that. "Where are we even going?"

"Don't know. I just want to make sure we're not followed before we stop anywhere. Marisa might be able to set something up." He glanced over at her, smiling. "If you hadn't seen that light out the window, we could have been toast."

"It wasn't like I was keeping watch. I couldn't sleep so I got up. I was having crazy dreams about bank security systems."

Hollis looked down at the gauges on his dashboard. He drew his mouth into a tight thin line. "The car is almost out of gas. We'll have to stop."

Laura tensed and then craned her neck to

look out the back window. Two cars were behind them.

Hollis drove for a while longer before turning off the main road and zigzagging through
town. He came back out on the main road. As
they neared the city limits, he hit the blinker
and turned into an open gas station on the edge
of town.

He pulled up to the pump. "Stay in the car."

She had no intention of getting out.

There was no one else at the gas station at
this late hour. Through the large windows of the
building, she could see a younger-looking man
behind the counter. Several times, Hollis shoved
his credit card into the slot on the pump. He shook
his head and then pressed the pay-inside button.
He stepped inside to pay the clerk.

The delay made her nervous.

A car eased by on the road and then sped up.
She took in a breath.

Hollis returned and finished filling the gas
tank. The clerk pounded on the window and
waved a wallet.

Hollis slapped his forehead and then went
back into the store to get his wallet.

She watched him as he spoke to the clerk, took
to the wallet and turned toward the glass door.

A car pulled in between the store and gas
pumps. It inched forward but did not stop. Even

before the first bullet was fired, instinct told her she was in danger. She slipped down below the dashboard. Gunfire sprayed everywhere and glass rained down.

Though it was probably only a matter of seconds, the shooting seemed to go on forever. Not trusting the hush that followed, she remained on the floor of the car, trembling and taking in quick sharp breaths.

When she finally did look out the window, she saw that the robbers had not only shot up the car, but also the glass door and windows of the store.

As she drew breath through her teeth, she didn't see Hollis anywhere. Was he okay?

Seconds before the windows shattered, Hollis had seen the semi-auto rifle resting on the open car window. He'd backed up and hit the ground as glass sprayed everywhere.

The assault lasted for maybe a few seconds. He heard the car engine roar and the vehicle speed away, tires squealing. He turned around.

Half rising from the floor and still not trusting that it was over, he turned back toward the counter. The clerk was not visible.

"You all right?" he called out.

"Yes," said a meek voice.

Fully aware that the men could come back,

he rushed outside toward the car. His worst fear was that Laura had not survived the attack. He flung open the driver-side door. Laura was crouched on the floor by the passenger side, resting her head and chest on the seat cushion. Her laced fingers covered the back of her head.

"Laura?"

She lifted her head as bits of glass fell from her hair and back.

"You're okay?"

"If you use the term *okay* loosely."

"You're not hit?"

"I don't think so."

He heard sirens in the distance. Someone must have seen the assault and called it in, or the clerk had.

He hurried around to the passenger side of the car, opened the door and gathered Laura into his arms. He held her close. She was trembling.

"I don't know how much more of this I can take," she said.

Two police cars pulled in to the gas station.

A police officer came toward them. Hollis released Laura from his embrace, but kept his arm wrapped around her waist. She pressed close to him. Hollis identified himself as an FBI agent, though he didn't have ID to show because he'd been undercover.

The officer tilted his head to one side. His

raised an eyebrow and his tight-lipped expression indicated that he was skeptical.

"I don't know if you were involved with talking to Agent Phillips at the house on Crabapple Street across town, but she'll vouch for me."

The officer nodded. "Okay. We were just there."

"I can give you a description of the car that did this drive-by shooting." They had probably already left town, but maybe the highway patrol could catch up with them if they remained on the highway. That was a big *if*. The robbers were cunning and would probably find a back-road route or a hiding place.

The officer pulled out his notebook and took Hollis's description of the car. Then he walked over to his patrol car and got on his radio. The other policeman was talking to the clerk.

The safest place for them to be right now would be the police station until he could coordinate with Agent Phillips to find a car and an alternative place for Laura to stay.

The officer returned to talk to them. "Would the two of you like to come down to the police station to make a statement?"

Both of them nodded. They got in the back of the patrol car and sat close together.

Neon and traffic lights clicked by in his peripheral vision on the drive to the station. He entwined his hand with Laura's, hoping that would bring her some comfort. She had barely spoken since the attack.

The police station was quiet at this hour. There were ten desks in the administrative area but only two officers present. Hollis and Laura gave their statements in separate rooms.

Hollis felt a weariness as he called Agent Phillips and let her know the situation.

After listening, Marisa responded. "It will take me until tomorrow to get you a car and longer to find a safe place for Laura. We might be looking at flying her out of state at this point."

He doubted Laura would like that. She wanted to go back to her life and her work. But even if they were able to set up some protection for her, given the nature of the attacks, the threat level was just too high.

Laura came out of the room where she'd been interviewed. They both sat in stunned silence for quite a while.

The officer who had driven them to the station got off the phone and walked over to them. "Can I arrange for you folks to have a ride somewhere?"

"Is there some out-of-the-way place we could stay? Nothing conspicuous like a hotel."

Even if the robbers did come back to town looking for them, there would not be a car that would give away their location. But he wasn't about to take any chances.

The officer thought about it for a moment, hooking his fingers into his gun belt. "There's a vacation rental nearby. I can check and see if it's vacant. The lady that owns it lives next door. I hate to roust her out of bed to get it unlocked, but I bet she would appreciate the money."

The officer checked on his computer and then made a phone call before walking back over to Hollis and Laura. "I can take you there."

As they walked out to the police car, Hollis addressed the officer. "Could you arrange for your nighttime patrol guys to go by the place a few times until morning?"

"Not a problem," said the officer. "You think those guys might come back?"

"It's not a chance we can take."

They got into the car and drove deeper into the residential part of town until they came to a large lot that had a bungalow-style house with a detached garage, and a tiny house that glowed with golden light.

"Looks like Mavis turned the lights on for you," said the officer. "She said she would unlock it for you. You can pay her in the morning."

The officer waited while they got out of the car and trudged up the little stone walkway. They stepped inside the tiny house, where lights were strung across the high ceiling and a small Christmas tree was placed by the window that looked out on the street. On the windowsill was a miniature Nativity set.

The main floor was maybe ten by twenty with a ladder that led to a loft area. The place gave off a cozy vibe despite feeling a little chilly.

Laura sat down on the sofa, which faced the kitchen area. "I'm still pretty wound up. I don't think I can go to sleep."

Hollis wandered over to the small woodstove, where a pile of wood was stacked neatly beside it. "We need to warm the place up, anyway."

She took the two steps to where the stove and sink were and opened the cupboards. "I can make us some tea."

"That sounds good." Hollis used the newspaper by the stove as kindling and then built a teepee of the thinner logs around that. He lit the fire and watched it burst into a dancing orange glow. He looked over his shoulder.

Laura had a kettle on and two mugs sat on the counter. "Hollis, I want to talk to you about an idea that I had."

Once the fire was going, Hollis tossed a large log on it and closed the door. A little place like this would not take long to heat up.

When he turned back around, Laura was sitting on the couch again.

He came and sat beside her. "What is it you want to talk about?" He noticed that she had picked up the Baby Jesus from the Nativity and was turning it around in her hand. Maybe the fidgeting was helping her deal with her nerves.

She put the little figurine on the side table by the couch and turned to face him. "I've been thinking that I might be able to help more with this case if I could see the security systems of the banks that were robbed, or at least walk through and examine the layouts."

"You mean look at the schematics for the security systems? With the permission of the banks, we might be able to get those."

"That might help, but I need to go to the banks themselves. We know this guy finds a way to case the bank for some time. He must be looking for vulnerabilities other than just figuring out how to disable the security systems."

"What do you mean?"

"For example, if he scouted out the bank where I was, he would have realized that only two tellers open up and one of them was an older woman."

"I guess that would have made it an easier target." Hollis thought about the implications of what she was saying. "It's not a bad idea. I would go with you. I know the details of each of the robberies and can walk you through it."

They would be out in the open, but the risk of returning to a bank that had already been robbed was probably pretty low.

"Maybe tomorrow we can go to the one that's the closest to here."

"Sure, the third robbery took place in a town about forty miles from here." Hollis pulled out his phone. "Which reminds me, I need to call Agent Phillips and let her know where to have the car dropped off at."

The kettle whistled. While Hollis stepped away to make his phone call, Laura jumped up to prepare the tea.

As he clicked in the number to reach Marisa, he debated Laura's plan. Would her idea help bring the case to a close, so she could return to her life, or would he be putting her in danger that could end her life?

FIFTEEN

Laura selected two tea bags and poured the hot water into the mugs. Hollis was still talking on the phone. The call to Marisa had been brief and now it sounded like he was conversing with some sort of supervisor, running her idea by him.

The couch had two narrow shelves on either side of it. She put Hollis's steaming mug on a shelf and then sat down on the other end of the couch. After taking a sip of tea, she set her mug by the Baby Jesus figurine she'd picked up earlier.

At one time, she had believed that the Savior of the world had shown up in the world as a vulnerable baby. Maybe it had been just all the warmth and magic and promise of happy family time that had made her like Christmas so much. Somehow that had gotten all mixed up in her young mind. What did she believe now?

Hollis clicked off his phone and sat down beside her. "So my supervisor at the Bureau is going to get back to me on your idea."

"Do you think it will work?"

"It's worth a try, but only if we can ensure your safety."

"I wouldn't be in any more danger than I have been all along. They find us no matter what."

"True."

She took a guess at why there was an edge to his voice. "Hollis, it's not your fault. That man and his thugs have been relentless."

"Thanks for saying that. All the same, putting a civilian in danger is not my idea of doing my job."

She turned and stared at the man in front of her, meeting his gaze. Hollis was the biggest reason she had begun to ask herself if she'd been wrong to shut God out of her life. He had shown her what it meant to be dependent on God in a crisis.

She picked up the plastic Baby Jesus and stared at it. "I've been thinking."

He leaned toward her. "About the deeper meaning of Christmas?"

"Years ago, when I was just a kid, I prayed to God all the time that He would make it so I wouldn't be so lonely because it was just me and my dad. When that prayer wasn't answered, I think my heart closed off to Him," said Laura.

Hollis's voice filled with compassion. "That is a hard thing to go through as a kid and then to feel like God didn't show up for you."

"I never realized that that was what I did. There was a point at which I felt betrayed by God. Really, I hadn't even thought about it until you prayed when we were trying to get to safety on that mountain…and then I found myself saying prayers."

"Sometimes we have to get to a desperate place to realize we need God."

"I think I should give God another chance." She looked away from the figurine and turned her head toward Hollis. The warmth and honesty she saw in his expression drew her in.

"I think that's a beautiful idea."

He wrapped his arms around her and drew her close, kissing her on the temple. He let go of her and scooted away, perhaps recognizing the impulsivity of the kiss.

"Sorry. I'm just happy for you," he said.

She laughed and so did he. She hadn't minded the gesture at all. She found herself wishing for more.

He grabbed his mug and took a sip of tea. "This is really good."

"It's chamomile. It's supposed to help you sleep."

"Let's hope it does the trick. My body is dead

tired, but my mind wants to run a marathon," Hollis said.

"I know that feeling."

They finished their tea. The small space had grown warm from the fire. Hollis pointed toward the loft. "Why don't you take that bed up there?" He patted the couch. "I'll sleep down here."

Laura splashed some water on her face in the little bathroom and then climbed the ladder to the loft. She peered over the edge to see that Hollis had located some blankets and a pillow. "Good night."

He smiled up at her. "Good night."

He removed his holster and placed the gun on one of the little shelves where he could grab it quickly. A bitter reminder of the threat they were still under.

Laura settled beneath the warm fluffy comforter and stared at the night sky through the skylight.

Good night, God. See You in the morning. Hope we can talk some more then.

She drifted off to sleep, waking hours later to the aromas of cinnamon and coffee floating in the air. She climbed down from the loft.

"Good morning," said Hollis. "Mavis, the lady who owns this place, gave me some fresh-baked cinnamon rolls when I went over to pay her."

"Sounds yummy." She went into the bathroom to freshen up, wishing she had a change of clothes or at least a toothbrush. Her suitcase had been left in the parking lot after the explosion, and somewhere she'd lost track of her phone and purse.

When she stepped into the main area, Hollis held up a mug. "Coffee?"

"Sure."

"How do you like it?"

"A teaspoon of sugar is great, thank you."

Hollis had already put his shoulder holster back on. Despite how cozy the morning felt, she knew it was an illusion. He handed her the steaming mug after stirring in the sugar. "Cinnamon rolls are still warm. Want one?"

"Sure."

She sat down with her coffee. Hollis handed her a paper plate with the aromatic roll on it.

Hollis was still wearing the clothes he'd gotten at his aunt and uncle's place.

"I could use some toiletries and a change of clothes. You probably could, too."

"Marisa has arranged for the car to be dropped off. I asked her to pick up a few things."

When she pulled the cinnamon roll apart, steam rose up from it. It almost melted in her mouth. "Great way to start the day." She tasted her coffee. "Have you heard from your supervisor yet?"

Hollis took a sip of coffee. "He thinks it can't hurt to at least have you go to the bank in Wilson. That's the closest one."

"It's unlikely they would hit the same bank a second time. That would break a pattern."

"True. I just don't know about you being out in the open."

They finished eating. Hollis grabbed his empty mug and put it in the sink. He pulled aside the curtain and looked out the window above the sink. "Looks like the car is here. Whoever dropped it off must have just left it and gotten their ride back. If it had been Marisa, she would have at least said hello." He stepped toward the door.

"I'll help you carry the stuff in." She moved to get up from where she was sitting.

"It would be best if you stayed inside for now."

She sat back down. She knew Hollis was just playing it safe. They were still in the same town where the drive-by shooting had taken place. But if the suspects had been watching the police station and saw them leave, it seems like they would have struck by now.

Hollis went outside and closed the door behind him.

Laura waited, listening to the sound of the clock ticking on the wall. They had to assume that no place was safe. Remaining hypervigilant was the only way they would survive.

Hollis glanced around the residential neighborhood as he approached the car. The winter chill stung his skin. He checked underneath the car for any sign of an explosive. He peered through the window. There was a large bag on the passenger seat. He opened the door and grabbed the bag.

He wished that whoever had dropped off the car would have spoken to him. He checked the glove box for the car keys but found none. They weren't underneath the car mat, either. After a quick survey of the neighborhood, he stepped toward the tiny house.

There wasn't much activity this early in the morning. A man navigated the icy sidewalk to his car and another pulled away from the curb. Other than that, the neighborhood was quiet. No matter what, he knew he couldn't let down his guard, despite the serenity of the morning.

Hollis stepped into the tiny house, where Laura sat sipping her coffee. The smile she offered him made his heart beat faster.

He felt a bond with her that went deeper than friendship, or even working together to solve this case. Until she recommitted to God, he had closed off that part of himself that wanted to see her in a romantic way. Everything was different this morning. He found himself wishing that their lives were in a more settled, less dangerous place.

Hollis looked in the bag and found clothing for him and Laura, toiletries and his FBI credentials. He would have to show them when they went to the bank. Without a warrant, which would take some time, anything the bank manager showed them would have to be voluntary.

"You can shower first if you want. I'm still working on my second cup of coffee and waking up," said Laura.

"Sounds good." He pulled her clothes out of the bag and set them to one side. The keys for the car were at the bottom.

Hollis showered and got into the clothes that had been provided for him—a button-down shirt, dress slacks and long wool coat, the official uniform of FBI agents that weren't undercover. A far cry from the camo jeans and black T-shirts he'd worn when he was trying to infiltrate the robbery ring. Hollis combed through his wet hair and stepped back into the tiny living space.

Laura's expression brightened. "You clean up nice."

Laura had found a radio station that was playing Christmas songs. As the music spilled out of the speaker, he found himself remembering what this time of year was all about. About twenty minutes later, Laura emerged from the bathroom dressed in a royal blue blouse and navy slacks. She looked beautiful. He handed her the coat that had been provided for her.

They locked up the house and got into the car. Mavis, an older woman with salt-and-pepper hair, waved at them from the window of the big house. Hollis started the car and let out a sigh. Back to business.

Hollis found himself wishing that it was Sunday and that he and Laura were on their way to church or some sort of Christmas celebration. Not working a case and dodging killers.

Laura asked a question, which stirred him from his thoughts. "I suppose other agents have interviewed all the people who were at the robberies?"

"Yes," he said. "There are summary reports that we can access at the field offices as well as recordings of the interviews. I've read them at least three times so I'll be able to fill you in while we're at the bank."

The miles clicked by quickly as they drove to the bank in Wilson, where the robbery had taken place. Hollis pulled into the lot, where a city police car was already parked.

As they got out, the officer waved at them

from behind the wheel. Banks this small usually didn't have security guards. Hollis let Laura step in front of him. The town of Wilson was only a couple of thousand people surrounded by agricultural land and farms.

He found himself taking note of all the cars and pedestrians as he walked in behind her. Laura seemed equally agitated, yet she proceeded. He had a deep appreciation for her fortitude and courage.

Once inside the bank, Laura tilted her head, probably assessing where the cameras were placed.

There were two tellers on duty, one dealing with customers in the drive-through. Hollis didn't recognize either of them as having been present at the time of the robbery. It would have been nice to ask if the tellers who had witnessed the robbery remembered any workman in the bank in the days leading up to the event.

"When did this robbery happen?" Laura turned toward him.

"Two p.m. on a Wednesday if I remember correctly. All the robberies were different times of day, different days of the week."

"I wonder why those times were chosen," said Laura.

"We haven't been able to answer that question with any clarity." He ushered Laura toward a glass-walled office, where a man was sitting at his desk. "The bank manager is expecting us. We'll start with him."

The bank manager looked up from his computer as they approached. He pushed back his chair and met them at the open door. His name was on the door—Nathan Miller.

Hollis showed his badge. "I'm FBI Special Agent Hollis Pryce. This is Laura Devin. She's a security expert. Mr. Miller, we have some questions for you."

"Please come in and sit down. I've been expecting you. You can call me Nathan. I want to get to the bottom of these robberies as much as you do."

Hollis entered the office after Laura, praying that this interview would help end the dangerous nightmare they both found themselves in.

As he sat down, he could see the city cop pulling out of the lot. He must have had to take another call. All the same, the lack of extra protection played on his already frayed nerves.

The weight of his gun in the shoulder holster reminded Hollis that he was prepared to save Laura and the bank employees if it came to that, even if it cost him his life.

SIXTEEN

Not sure how to proceed, Laura took a chair beside Hollis as the bank manager sat back down. She really wanted to look at their security system from the inside out, but it didn't seem like that should be the first thing she addressed. Best to build some trust first. Besides, there was something that was dancing around the corners of her thoughts. The varied times and dates of the robberies couldn't be random.

She asked the first question. "Were you here the day your bank was robbed?"

Nathan shook his head. "Unfortunately, no, I was down with the flu, as was another teller."

Hollis jumped in. "So you were short-staffed on the day of the robbery?"

Nathan ran his hands through his thinning hair. "Yes, with two of us out, there were two tellers in the morning and only one in the afternoon."

Again, the human element seemed to be a factor in when the robberies occurred.

"Were you busy that day in terms of the number of transactions and customers?"

"It was a Wednesday, which is normally a slower day. Our busy days are Fridays and, of course, the day after a bank holiday," said Nathan.

"But there was an unusual amount of cash taken in," Hollis said.

"Yes, three of the major merchants in town make a deposit on Wednesday at noon." Nathan looked over his shoulder. "Looks like my next appointment is here, if you don't mind. I'm also the chief loan officer. I can answer more questions later if you like."

Laura turned and craned her neck. A young couple sat in the chairs outside the office flipping through magazines. Maybe she wasn't going to get an insider's look at the security system.

Laura turned back to face Nathan as he was standing up. "Do you mind if we look around the bank?"

"No, of course not." Nathan was already headed toward the door. "Anything to help catch the guys who robbed us."

Hollis and Laura stepped out into the lobby, where the two tellers were behind the counter.

"It's clear that the man who plans these robberies waits for the time when there is the least amount of staff," said Hollis.

"With this bank he knew there would be a

large amount of cash because of the merchant deposits. With the bank in Clark River, the thieves wanted to get into the vault. They must have had intel that something of value was in there." Laura tilted her head to look at where the cameras were placed. Most security companies had similar protocols for where the cameras were mounted to provide the maximum amount of coverage.

Hollis leaned close to her. "What are you thinking?"

"Beefed-up security, what I was hired to assess, may not have prevented these robberies," she said.

"There is no way one man could be watching several banks day after day, waiting for the most vulnerable time. The man you saw on that screen must get some help from his thugs," said Hollis.

"Branson is the most likely one to have helped out with that, right?"

"Yes, he was clearly the guy in charge for the circle of thieves I managed to infiltrate," said Hollis.

"Did any of the other undercover agents obtain any useful information?"

Hollis shook his head. "I was the only one who managed to get on a robbery crew. The other undercover guys would make connections to the criminal class and start dropping hints about needing money and they'd be frozen out."

"Both you and I were around Branson long enough to recognize him on a camera even if he was trying to avoid it," said Laura. "Maybe we should look at some more of that footage."

"If we had just one decent face shot of either Branson or that other guy, it would go a long way to figuring out who they are," said Hollis. "And what their connection to each other is."

Laura felt like they were grasping at straws. "I'll do whatever it takes to end this, but it feels like we're taking the scenic route to try to bring the theft ring down."

"It's a complex case with lots of working parts. Maybe if we get Branson into custody, we can get him to squeal on his boss."

"You'd almost have to have another robbery take place and be ready for it in order to have that happen, right?"

Hollis nodded. "And we don't want that to happen."

"Did anything come from questioning Joe?"

"No, low-level guys don't know anything useful. They take their cut of the money and run. Then different guys are recruited for another robbery. We think that some of the same guys may have been in on more than one robbery, but honestly, it's a rotating cast of characters."

They stepped outside. The strip mall where the bank was located also had a jewelry store, a pawn shop, a fabric store and a small café. Across the street was a farm-supply place. Two people were on the sidewalk next to the strip mall. An older woman entered the fabric store and a teenager sat on bench.

Hollis pointed toward the café. "Are you hungry?"

"Starving," she said.

"We'll get it to go, so we're not out in the open for long."

There was always a reminder that they were not out of danger. Every precaution needed to be exercised.

As they headed toward the café, Laura said, "How long would it take to set up looking at some more footage?"

"No time at all, but we'd need to return to the Bozeman field office. They have the setup to access that information."

As they headed toward the café, a man emerged from the jewelry store. He met Laura's gaze momentarily and then looked away before disappearing into the pawn shop. Laura tensed. The man's expression had seemed almost hostile. Maybe the guy was just an unfriendly local. In a town this small, outsiders like her and Hollis were easy enough to spot.

They entered the café. As it was well past the lunch hour, there was only a mom with two kids at one of the four tables.

An older waitress stood behind the counter. "What can I do for you two?"

Hollis stepped forward. "We'd like to get a couple of meals to go. What do you have that's fast and good?"

"We can do you up a quick club sandwich. Comes with potato chips and a drink."

Hollis looked at Laura to see if she was okay with the meal choice. She nodded at him.

"That sounds good."

The waitress pointed toward a cooler. "Pick any of the drinks on the second shelf. I'll have the sandwiches out to you in a jiffy."

They waited for less than five minutes before the waitress brought out two to-go containers. She rang up the food and Hollis paid with a credit card.

Once they got out to the car, they headed out of town. The light snow that was falling intensified and Hollis turned on the windshield wipers.

"Think I'll just pull over. Too hazardous to try to eat and drive," Hollis said.

Laura's stomach growled. She hadn't wanted to seem rude and start eating when he couldn't. After driving for a few miles, he turned onto a gravel road that must lead to a farm or something. He kept the car running so the heat blasted but turned off the wipers.

She handed him his container. "Thank you for paying for the meal. If I hadn't lost my purse, I would have paid for my share."

"No worries. The Bureau will foot the bill for it," Hollis said. He opened his container. "Should we say grace together?"

Her heart fluttered. "Yes, I'd like that. Why don't you say it?"

He reached over and took her hand. They both closed their eyes. "Lord, we thank You for this meal. Thank You for the good company. Please keep us safe. We love You."

"Amen," she said. There was something wonderful about praying with Hollis.

They ate their meal while the snow filled up the windshield, blocking their view but creating a sort of cozy, closed-in feeling.

In between bites, he reached over and turned on the wipers when the snow started to pile up.

Though hot soup would have been wonderful on such a cold day, the sandwich tasted good. She took a sip of the lemonade she'd chosen. "That was nice praying together."

Hollis took his last bite of sandwich, wiped his mouth and smiled. "Maybe there'll be more prayers together in the future."

His remark caused an electric shock to zing through her. Her cheeks grew hot. "Yes…maybe."

He shifted the car into Drive not adding anything more. His words made her feel like she was floating on air, but also left her wondering. Was he suggesting that there could be something romantic between them? They were friends, for sure, but did he want more?

What did she want? She had resigned herself to singlehood a long time ago. But getting to know Hollis had made her reconsider that vow.

She studied Hollis's profile as he focused on the road and they climbed a hill. She wasn't even sure how to phrase the question that swirled through her head.

As he coasted downhill, Hollis's expression suddenly changed. Fear settled into his features. He glanced down and then back through the windshield.

"What is it?" Tension threaded around her torso.

"My brakes aren't working."

Hollis's heart pounded as he gripped the wheel. Sailing down the icy hill, the car increased in speed. The needle pushed past seventy. When he glanced ahead, the road leveled off, but they would be going a dangerous speed by the time they got to the bottom of the hill. He had no choice but to hold on. Though pumping the brakes was an act of futility, he did it, anyway, almost involuntarily.

Laura stared straight ahead, bracing one arm on the dashboard.

When the road finally leveled off, the car fishtailed and swerved into the other lane. If there had been a vehicle coming toward them, they would have crashed. He had to stop this car. He veered off the road, hoping the deep snow would slow them. He watched the needle drop as they coasted to a stop in the middle of a snow-filled field.

Laura let out a sharp breath and pressed her palm on her chest. "What just happened?"

He wasn't too sure himself. Brakes usually didn't stop working that dramatically. Usually, there was some kind of warning. He'd had brakes go out on his truck but that had been gradual.

"We'll have to call and have someone come pick us up." He pulled out his phone, still processing what had happened.

Laura pushed open the door. "I need to catch my breath."

He could see her through the window as she got out and bent over, clutching her stomach but not throwing up.

Hollis stared at his keypad for a long moment. He dialed Marisa. If he couldn't reach her, they'd have to be towed back to Wilson and wait for someone to come get them.

He was almost certain that his brakes had been tampered with. But when? If it had been while the car sat outside the tiny house, it seems like they would have failed much sooner.

Marisa picked up after the third ring. "Hollis, I was about to call you. You're not going to believe what we're dealing with."

"What are you talking about?"

"There was a jewelry store robbery in Stanburg. You know, where they have all the sapphires."

Hollis wasn't sure why Marisa was telling him this. He was still shaken from realizing he could have died in a car crash.

Marisa continued. "Sorry, I guess I need to explain. One of the robbers matched the description of the guy who called himself Soldier. The MO of the robberies matches that of the bank— quick and well planned. The thieves knew the layout of the place before they entered."

Hollis cleared his throat. "You think our guy is switching things up?"

"Could be. I'm on the scene of the robbery right now gathering info."

Because he was still in shock, Hollis could not form a coherent answer.

Agent Phillips spoke up. "Sorry, I jumped

right in there about the jewelry-store robbery. Why are you calling? Did things go okay at the bank in Wilson?"

"Listen, Laura and I are stranded on the road, maybe fifteen miles outside of Wilson," said Hollis. "We'll need another car and a ride back to the field office."

"Did the car break down?"

"No, something went wrong with the brakes. We need to have this car towed and looked at." He pushed open the car door and got out. He leaned over to get a look at the underside of the car, but snow filled the wheel well and he couldn't see anything. "I'm concerned that it might have been sabotage."

"I'm still at the crime scene. Can you give highway patrol a call? If it was sabotage, it's concerning."

Hollis stared at the serpentine parallel grooves that the car had made as it plowed through the field, and then out at the road, where not a single car had gone by. They were out in the middle of nowhere. It wouldn't be a good idea for him and Laura to stay here. "I'll call highway patrol."

"I'll let you know if we learn anything from this robbery," said Marisa.

Laura came around to where Hollis was standing. She still looked pale and shaken.

"That would be good. Maybe the jewelry-store

robbery is unrelated." Hollis hung up. He called highway patrol and explained the situation. When he hung up, Laura was staring at him.

Fear spread across her features. "A jewelry store was robbed?"

"Yes, in Stanburg. Similar MO to the banks. And there was a bank robbery there over a year ago. A man who looked like Soldier was spotted at the jewelry store." He stepped toward her. "Laura, what is it?"

She shook her head. "I don't know why it didn't register when we were back in Wilson."

Hollis reached out for her. "What are you talking about?"

"That guy coming out of the jewelry store. I thought the look he gave me was hostile, but it was actually surprise...or fear."

"Laura, what are you saying?"

Some distance away on the road, a car passed by, going way under the speed limit.

"Remember I said that I didn't have a clear memory of the man on the screen? But that if I saw him again, I might recognize him?"

A lump formed in Hollis's throat. "You think the guy at the jewelry store in Wilson is the same man who's behind the bank robberies?"

Now it made sense. He was probably casing a jewelry store while another was being robbed by his crew.

Out on the road, the car that had been going so slow had turned back around and pulled off above where they were stranded. A man dressed in a winter coat with a hood got out and stared in their direction.

A passing motorist who was about to offer help?

The man opened his back car door and reached in for something. Even before the man turned around, instinct told Hollis that something was not right.

He reached for Laura's hand. "We have to get out of here."

A look of confusion crossed Laura's features and then her gaze moved toward the road, where the man had pulled a rifle out of his car.

His heart pounded and adrenaline poured through his body. "Get to the front of the car for cover."

Hollis pulled his handgun out of the holster. He was one step behind Laura. The first shot was fired just as he ran toward the front bumper.

SEVENTEEN

Crouching by the front of the car, Laura felt as though she was being shaken from the inside. The first rifle shot zinged through the air and hit some part of the car.

Hollis moved in beside her. "You okay?"

She nodded even though she was far from okay.

Hollis took up a position at the end of the bumper so he could peer out.

Was this the man they had been tracking all this time?

She closed her eyes and braced for another rifle shot. Hollis steadied his gun by using the bumper as a rest.

All around them was a flat field of snow. The only other place to take shelter was a cluster of trees some distance away. They would not be able to run very fast in the deep snow. They were trapped.

"Is he coming this way?"

Hollis did not shift his focus. "Yes." He rolled his body away from the edge of the car as another shot broke the silence.

He leaned closer to her. "If he gets within range. I can take him out."

She knew that a handgun could not shoot as far as a rifle. The suspect would have to be very close in order for Hollis to have any degree of accuracy. Hollis being able to shoot before the suspect did was not a high probability.

After several seconds of silence, Hollis scooted to the end of the bumper and looked. He whirled back around. "Get to the side of the car."

Heart pounding, Laura scrambled around to the passenger side of the car. Hollis slipped in behind her. He lifted his head to peer through the windows. "He's still coming toward us in a wide arc."

He pressed his back against the car door, moving his attention toward the front end of the car.

Despite being dressed for winter, she felt the cold seep into her skin as she remained still. She stared at the back of Hollis's head as he held his gun, ready to fire. The silence seemed to drag on forever.

"Can you see him?"

Hollis shook his head.

If the gunman was going to take the shot, he should have taken it by now. Hollis peered through the windows again and then moved toward the front of the car and lifted his head above the hood. "I don't know where he's gone."

Laura glanced in the other direction, fearing that the suspect had found a way to sneak up on them from the rear. No sign of the shooter.

She hurried toward the back of the car to look out toward the road. The car the man had come in was gone. A highway patrol car had rolled up and parked. It seemed the gunman must have seen the approaching highway-patrol car and decided to flee.

She breathed a sigh of relief as a highway patrolman got out of the car and waved at her. She waved back.

"Hollis, I think we're okay." She rose to her feet and started back toward the road. Her boots sunk into the deep snow.

Hollis fell in beside her as she tried to hurry. When they got closer to the road, the snow was not as deep.

The patrolman stepped toward them. "I heard you two needed a ride."

"Can we see if we can catch a dark blue SUV that went that way?" Hollis pointed in the direction opposite from where the patrol car had come. Then he addressed his comment to Laura. "Did you actually see him pull away?"

"No, he was nowhere in sight when I got to the back of our car," Laura said. "He must have seen you coming down the hill."

"Let's go. Maybe we can still catch him." Hollis ushered her toward the car.

The patrolman answered. "Hop in. I can put a call in to the other highway patrol to be on the lookout for the car."

They both got into the back seat of the officer's car. Laura tried to ease the tension in her body by taking a deep breath. The car pulled away from the shoulder and gained speed. The officer got on the radio, relaying the description of the car and the direction it had gone.

While the back-and-forth on the radio continued, Hollis slipped his hand into hers. His touch had a calming effect on her. The chatter on the radio continued until they reached the city limits with no indication the suspect's car had even been spotted.

The guy was clever. He'd probably found a place to hide until the fever of the search subsided. He might even have a way to get a different car.

The patrolman turned his head slightly. "Where to?"

Hollis gave him the address of the field office. When they pulled into the lot, there were several other cars parked there, since there were other businesses in the same building. All the evidence of the car explosion had been cleaned up.

Hollis thanked the patrolman. He and Laura walked the short distance to the field-office door.

"Do you think the man I saw will figure out that this is where we've gone?" She turned in a half circle, not seeing anyone in the parking lot. The few cars on the street moved at a normal pace, none of the drivers looking in toward where they were standing. Still, she could not let go of the fear.

"Hard to say." Hollis checked the door, which was locked. He pulled out a key card and swiped it. "Agent Phillips must still be dealing with the jewelry-store robbery."

They entered the quiet office.

Hollis checked his phone. "Marisa texted that she should have things wrapped up in an hour or so."

Laura collapsed in one of the chairs in the reception area. "It was just pure coincidence that we encountered the suspect leaving that jewelry store. He was probably casing it for the next robbery, right?"

"Yes, but I doubt that's still the plan given that we're on to him," Hollis said.

"He went back to one of the towns where he'd pulled a bank robbery."

"I'm sure that was the fastest, most efficient thing to do. He already knew the layout of the town, so he would know the fastest escape routes for his crew and how quickly law enforcement would react. All he had to do was figure out the vulnerabilities of the jewelry store." Hollis sat down in the chair beside her.

Through the window, she saw that it was already growing dark. The sky looked like it had a gray mesh stretched over it.

Hollis ran his hand through his hair. "It does seem like he's escalating. I'm sure once they discovered that an undercover agent had penetrated his ranks, he was in a full-on panic."

Laura closed her eyes and rested her head on the back of the chair. "What do you suppose his plan is? Is he going to get as much money as he can and then disappear, lay low and then pop up in another part of the country?" She turned her head and opened her eyes.

Hollis shifted his weight and then stood up. He paced toward the door and then came back to where she was sitting. "It is hard to say what he'll do next." Hollis seemed nervous.

"Now that I've seen him again, maybe I

should try to come up with a better picture of him." With a little prompting from a sketch artist, she thought she would be able to bring a more complete image to life.

Hollis walked over to the window that looked out on the parking lot. Placing his hands on his hips, he half turned away from her.

"Hollis, what is it? What are you thinking?" She had to know why he seemed so tense and so distant.

"It may be that our suspect goes into hiding. I know one thing about him even though I have never met him. He's vengeful and he knows we're closing in on him. Laura, whether he does it himself or he sends thugs, he's gonna keep coming after us until we're both dead."

"Oh, Hollis, I didn't want to think about it. But it's clear that you're right." She rose to her feet and rushed toward him. "He's not going to stop coming after us." Her voice faltered.

Hollis shook his head. "I wish I could tell you differently."

Her expression communicated anxiety as she drew her eyebrows together. But then she met his gaze and her features softened. "I'm just glad I'm here with you now. So glad I got to know someone like you." She fell into his arms.

He embraced her, swaying as he held her

close. He buried his face in her hair. It felt so wonderful to hold her even though he knew it couldn't last.

He kissed her forehead and then tilted her chin so he could gaze into the depths of her eyes. His lips found hers. He kissed her gently and drew her even closer to deepen the kiss.

He pulled back and brushed a strand of hair behind her ear as he took in the warmth of her gaze and the comfort that being close to her provided. There were words whirling through his mind that he was unwilling to speak. They were not safe. This moment was so transitory. All the same, he would enjoy it as long as he could. He kissed her again.

The kiss was interrupted by his phone ringing. Laura stepped back so he could pull his phone from his coat pocket. The ID said it was Agent Phillips. He pressed the talk button.

"We've had another jewelry-store heist. That makes three stores now in less than half an hour. This guy is pulling out all the stops," Marisa said.

Judging from the background noise, Agent Phillips was driving. "Where? All in the same town?" It would be unusual for the small towns to be able to support more than one jewelry store.

"The last two happened in the business section in Lovell Heights."

The name did not register with Hollis. It certainly wasn't one of the places a previous robbery had occurred. "Where is that?"

"By the resort," Marisa said.

Marisa was talking about an exclusive members-only club that provided skiing in the winter and golf and hiking in the summer. The club attracted lots of out-of-state millionaires and celebrities. This was a change from the other jobs.

"Jewelry stores are not federal, so not technically our jurisdiction. Local cops are not used to this magnitude of crime. They could use our help and we have reason to be involved since one of the suspects matched Soldier's description," Marisa said. "The preliminary info suggests this MO is different, but I think our suspect is behind this. Can you get over here and look at the crime scene? I could use a second set of eyes."

"I can't leave Laura alone."

"Bring her along. We can have one of the city cops stand guard or take her to the city police station. I need your expertise, Hollis, to know if this is our guy."

Hollis glanced at Laura. He didn't have a lot of options. "Okay, but we don't have a car."

"Someone from the sheriff's department can help you." Marisa's voice dropped half an octave as she spoke more slowly. "What really concerns me is maybe he had this planned all along to go out with a bang before he goes into hiding. We might be looking at more robberies before the night is over."

Her words echoed through his brain. "It's hard to say what this guy has planned next, but I think we need to take steps to inform law enforcement in all the towns where there is a jewelry store, and maybe even pawn shops, that might be targeted."

"That's a good idea. Can you make those calls on the ride in? I am a little overwhelmed right now," said Marisa.

"Got it. We'll be there as fast as we can." Hollis hung up.

Laura had only heard one side of the conversation. "I take it we're going somewhere. More robberies?"

"Jewelry stores by the resort."

"Quite a switch from the small rural towns. I'm sure he got substantially more value for his planning."

The change in pattern bothered Hollis, but he wasn't sure what to make of it. "You'll have to come with me. We'll arrange for you to have some police protection until Agent Phillips and I are done."

She stepped toward him and reached out to rest her hand on his cheek. "Wish I could stay with you."

Her touch reminded him of the kisses they had shared only minutes ago. "Me, too."

He also wished this case was solved, with the mastermind behind these robberies in custody. But right now he had work to do to make that happen. He made the call to the sheriff's office and found someone who could drive them.

They waited only minutes until the headlights of the sheriff's car shone in the window.

Hollis escorted Laura to the car as snow cascaded from the sky. "We can sit together in the back seat if you like. I have to make some calls to local police departments."

The miles ticked by while they sat together holding hands. Hollis alerted the police departments in the small towns about his suspicions. The sheriff's car was the only one on the winding road to the resort. The business district was about six blocks long, with some side streets surrounded by condos. Larger, more expensive homes were farther up the mountain, and some looked out on the ski slopes and golf course.

The shops had been designed to look like something out of an old-world Italian village. Twinkling Christmas lights competed with the flashing lights on three police cars. An officer emerged from an unmarked car about a block away.

"Why don't you stay close to me until we

can get you some protection?" Hollis suggested. They walked toward where most of the activity seemed to be. The display window of the jewelry store was shattered.

Agent Phillips was inside talking with one of the local police officers. When she saw Hollis and Laura, she walked over to them.

"Glad you made it. We've already done a preliminary look at the other two stores."

Hollis pointed toward the broken window. "Were both robberies after-hours smash and grabs?" That wasn't like the banks at all or the jewelry store in Wilson. This might be an unrelated crime.

Laura stepped toward Hollis. "The alarms would have gone off right away."

"The robberies were almost simultaneous," Marisa said. "The last two of the jewelry stores are within blocks of each other. We're thinking a crew of maybe four to six men. Not many people around once the shops close. The uniformed officers are canvassing to see if we can stir up any witnesses."

Hollis studied the crime scene. "This isn't one of the places where a bank was robbed. The target and the MO are different. What if this isn't even our guy?"

Laura stepped closer to Marisa. "But I know that was him coming out of that jewelry store in Wilson. It may not be a certain link, but it suggests a connection."

"And the Stanburg jewelry-store robbery was more his style." He had a feeling Laura was right, but why the change and the frantic increase in robberies? "We might as well gather as much evidence and information as we can. If nothing else, it'll help the locals with their investigation."

Marisa turned to face Laura. "I told them you needed extra protection. One of the officers should be here shortly once they notice that you arrived."

Laura nodded. "I'll let you guys do your thing. If you don't mind, I'd like to look at the alarm system." She pointed toward a sign on the broken window. "I know that company. Pretty standard stuff. The alarm goes off and it's relayed to a company operator, who then alerts the local police."

"What would that create? A few minutes' delay in the cops being informed and then whatever time it takes them to get to the scene?" Hollis began to walk around the store, taking in everything, but was careful not to disturb anything before the crime-scene crew showed up.

Marisa had moved toward the broken display cases.

Laura remained closer to the door. A uniformed officer came up to her and tapped her on the shoulder, speaking too softly for Hollis to hear. The officer stepped back onto the sidewalk.

Laura took one step toward Hollis. "Officer Christie says he can take me to the police station."

"Sounds good. We'll probably end up there, anyway, to compare notes with the local officers. I'll see you in a bit." Hollis's attention was still on the results of the robbery as Laura stepped out to the sidewalk and was enveloped by the darkness.

Minutes later, the out-of-town crime-scene crew showed up. Marisa met Hollis out on the sidewalk and a uniformed policeman approached them.

"We may have a witness who was coming home from a bar. He didn't see the robbery, but he saw men get out of a vehicle on this street," said the police officer.

"Can he describe the men?" If any of them matched Soldier's or Branson's description that would be a solid link back to the bank robberies.

"He saw their faces briefly and from a distance. He was headed back to his house up a side street when the robberies happened. The alarms were silent. He came forward when he looked out his window and saw all the police cars."

"Can we speak to the witness?" Hollis wondered if the man had been close enough to see if any of the men had a neck tattoo.

"We took him to the station to see if looking at mug shots might jar his memory."

"I'll go talk to him. I need to go to the station, anyway. Officer Christie escorted a witness there to keep her safe."

The officer did a double take and then shifted his weight. "There's no Officer Christie on the Heights police force."

"Then who...?" A lump formed in his throat. Images rushed by Hollis in his peripheral vision. It felt as though he were being pulled backward through a tunnel.

Marisa grasped his arm. "Hollis, are you okay?"

He shook his head. "This was all a setup to lure us out."

"What are you talking about?"

"The suspect has kidnapped Laura." Hollis's mouth had gone dry. "She may already be dead."

EIGHTEEN

From the passenger seat of the squad car, Laura stared out the windshield as the darkened shops clipped by.

Officer Christie approached the outskirts of town and took an abrupt left. They passed a city park and then there was forest on either side of the road.

"Is this the way to the police station?"

Officer Christie stared at the road. "Just relax."

The back of her neck tingled, an involuntary fear response. Up ahead, she saw no sign of any kind of building, not even lights that would be from a house. She tried to come up with a rational explanation. "Is the police station outside of town?"

The car picked up speed once they left the city limits. "Everything is going to be okay."

The inflection in the man's voice lacked reassurance. In fact, his words held a threatening tone. "I think I'd like to go back to where the other officers are." Her hand reached for the door handle.

"I bet you would." The driver pressed on the accelerator as they headed down what had become a dark country road.

Despite the uniform and the squad car, she knew now that this man had sinister intent. He was no police officer. Panic set in as she gripped the door handle.

The whooshing rhythm in her ears from her heart pounding intensified. When she craned her neck, she could no longer see the lights of the town. "What is this about? Where are you taking me?"

The man at the wheel did not reply.

"Please let me out."

His response was to go even faster as the road went gradually uphill. The darkness covered the forest. The trees became one big silhouette. Only the headlights provided a view of where they were going. She saw a cattle guard up ahead. The driver would have to slow down for that, providing her with her only chance for escape.

Maybe if she kept him talking, he'd be distracted enough for her plan to work. "Who do you work for? The man who did those robberies?" This must be the police car stolen from Clark River.

He remained silent and maintained a steady speed. The cattle guard almost seemed to catch him by surprise as he ran over it. The car jerked and bumped. Once on the other side of it, he eased off the gas for only a second. This was her chance. She pushed open the door and jumped.

She hit the ground hard and rolled. Feeling as though she had been beaten with sticks, she stopped, landing on her stomach. Behind her, the car idled with its headlights still on. When she heard the car door slam, she pushed herself to her feet despite the pain. She stumbled toward the trees and turned downhill. When she grew fatigued and out of breath, she slowed to a jog. In the darkness, her foot caught on a root. Her knees took the brunt of the fall, though pain vibrated through her legs.

She looked over her shoulder, not seeing anything. Only the wind rushing through the trees broke the silence around her. It was not possible the man would just give up and not chase her. She set out at a slower pace, still tuning her senses to her surroundings, listening for any noise that might be out of place.

After she had walked for what felt like a very long time, the darkness had become disorienting. She wasn't even sure she was going in the right direction. She had no cell phone. Sometime after the explosion she had lost track of it. All the trees that surrounded her looked the same.

She turned to where she thought the road might be. The man in the police uniform might be waiting for her to come out, but she had to get a view of where she was. She walked for at least ten minutes, unable to get out of the forest. She was lost.

The night had grown colder, making the skin on her face tingle. Fighting off despair, she kept going. It appeared that the man hadn't followed her, but why not?

As she walked, she heard an odd sound above her, like electric crickets. She tilted her head. Above her, she saw a tiny flashing light that angled and zoomed away. A drone.

Her heart pounded and she burst into a sprint. That was how the man would locate her. Panicked, she thought hiding would be the better option. But she'd freeze if she spent the night out here.

Once Hollis and Marisa returned to the police station they would figure out she'd been kidnapped and they'd have to send out search parties in all directions. But would help come out to this deserted stretch? She couldn't count on them finding her before the man in the police uniform did. Her only choice was to keep moving in what felt like the right direction.

Even though she had on good winter boots, it didn't take long for her feet to start feeling numb, along with her face and fingers. How long before frostbite set in?

She came to what looked like a hiking trail. It had to lead somewhere, she reasoned, and set out on it. Again, she heard the drone above her.

Keep moving.

She repeated the phrase over and over. The words transformed into *God, help me.*

The trail faded. It hadn't been a trail at all, just a worn path the deer had probably created. It was a strain to put one foot in front of the other. She lifted her head. Her heart pounded.

A man who was more shadow than substance stood in front of her.

Instinct to survive gave her the energy to flee. The man's footsteps were right behind her. His hand grabbed her and pulled her backward. She angled her body to get away and kicked at the same time. Her feet hit him as he lifted her off the ground. She flailed her legs. Her head hit something solid and then everything went dark.

Once he realized Laura had been kidnapped, it had taken Hollis less than twenty minutes to organize three search parties. Each one took one of the roads that led out of the resort. He, a city officer and Marisa took the road that led to some private homes up the mountain. At the edge of town, they stopped at residences by the park and knocked on doors. They found a witness who had seen a police car headed up the road less than twenty minutes ago.

That had to be their guy.

Hollis instructed the city officer to get on the radio and redirect the other search parties to this area.

Once the city cop finished talking on the radio, Hollis asked him, "Is there anything else up this road besides private homes?"

"All the residences connect to a lodge at the top of the ski hill. Some homes are walking distance to it and some are farther back in the hills."

"How many homes are we talking about?"

"Twenty or so. All on large lots," said the police officer.

Hollis stared through the car window at the darkness outside.

"Guess we start knocking on doors again," said Marisa from the back seat. "Maybe somebody saw something."

That was probably the best option. It was past 8:00 p.m. Most people would still be awake. He addressed his question to the policeman. "How many miles are we talking about covering here?"

The officer shrugged. "Those homes are really spread out. Some of them are way back in the mountains."

Hollis felt a tightening in his chest as he tried to form the words to ask the next question. "Is there a secluded place where someone might take a person to kill them, where there would be no danger of a witness?"

The police officer rubbed his chin. "Lot of dense forest around here."

Hollis figured their best plan would be to get a helicopter to conduct a search. But it would take too long to get one out here.

A chill permeated his skin. He feared the worst. Once the kidnapper got Laura to a secluded placc, there would be no reason to keep her alive.

NINETEEN

Laura came to in darkness beneath a warm quilt on a comfortable bed. Her mind could not process where she was. She reached out for where she thought a light might be. Once turned on, the nightstand lamp revealed that she was in a bedroom that looked like it belonged in a bed-and-breakfast. It was done up in a country chic style, with antique furniture and pictures of landscapes on the wall.

She tossed back the covers. She was still in her clothes, but she didn't see her coat, boots or gloves anywhere.

She moved toward the door, expecting it to be locked. She saw that her boots were by the door and she put them on. When she reached for the doorknob, it twisted in her hand. Not locked. She stepped into a large living room with a circular couch. An expansive window looked out on the valley, which was dotted with lights here and there that must have been homes.

Far in the distance, she saw the clustered lights of a small city.

Noise was coming from somewhere deeper in the house, but not in an adjacent room.

Her memory started to work. She'd been kidnapped, knocked unconscious and brought here. She rushed toward sliding doors that led to a balcony. It was locked from the outside. She checked the other door, which led to another bedroom and a library.

She hurried into the library. When she slid one of the windows open, a blast of cold air hit her. She peered down. It looked as if she was on the top floor of a three-story log cabin. She pressed against the screen, seeking to remove it. It would be risky to go into the night with no coat but she had to try. Maybe she could get to one of those other houses.

A voice boomed behind her. "I wouldn't try that if I were you. It's a long way down. You could break a leg."

Laura whirled around. The man she'd viewed on the screen, the same one she'd seen coming out of the jewelry store, smiled at her.

Her heartbeat intensified as he stepped toward her and slammed the window shut. His gaze probed her. He was standing close enough that she could smell his oppressive cologne. He was clean-cut, lean, maybe in his early forties.

The droopy eyelid was the only thing distinctive about him.

She took a step back. He grabbed her arm, squeezing to the point of pain. His lip curled back as he spoke, revealing perfect veneers. "You don't want to break your leg now, do you, Laura?"

"You're hurting me." There was only one reason why this man was showing himself to her. She was trapped with no chance of escape and his intention was to kill her. Why the delay, she was not sure. The thug who had caught her in the forest could have broken her neck and ended it right there.

He let go of her arm but made a point of lifting his jacket so she had a view of the shoulder holster with the gun. "Please, come sit down. You must be hungry."

She could not process this strange show of hospitality. All the same, she followed him back into the living room. Her gaze darted everywhere.

A tray containing cheese, lunch meat and crackers had been placed on the coffee table by the couch, along with two bottles of water.

"Please have a seat." The man sat in front of the tray, then grabbed a small paper plate and placed food on it. "Help yourself. I know I'm starving."

She sat as far away as she could from him. Her eyes were still taking in her surroundings.

The man took a bite of cheese. "Every door on this floor is locked from the outside in case you are wondering."

"Why haven't you killed me yet? That's what you intend to do, right?"

"Several reasons. I need to be as far away from here as I can be when it happens."

"They'll know that you live up here," said Laura.

"It's a vacation rental, my dear. Rented under the name of Arthur Richards—not my real name, mind you." He scooted toward her on the couch and leaned close. "After all this time, you must know that I don't overlook a single detail."

"Of course, I know that," Laura said. "Those last two jewelry-store robberies were a little out of form though. Smash and grab, total lack of planning."

His eye that was droopy twitched and he raised his chin. She now realized the only weakness of the man who was currently going by the name of Arthur Richards. Pride.

"I did that on purpose. I thought something so over-the-top would get you and that agent out of your hiding place." He drew his eyes into narrow piercing slits. "And it did."

She and Hollis had been lured into this trap.

A horrifying realization sunk into her brain. "You're keeping me alive until you can get Hollis, too."

Arthur's face turned red and he jerked to his feet. "No one crosses me like that Hollis Pryce did." Every word the man spoke was filled with rage.

He picked up the water bottle, took a gulp and slammed it back down on the table. "Unfortunately, your agent friend brought a little army with him to search for you. The drone and my men are just waiting for him to be separated long enough to grab him."

He cleared his throat. "And now I have to pack. I've got a long flight ahead of me." Arthur left the room.

She heard voices and before she could even stand up, Branson entered the room, a gun clearly visible on his hip. "Laura Devin, good to see you again."

Laura felt as though a weight was on her chest and all the air was being sucked out of her lungs. She was looking at the man who was probably going to kill her and Hollis.

"How long has that man who goes by Arthur been staying here? Someone must have seen him in town. They will link him back to this cabin when our bodies are found."

Branson snorted. "He's not sloppy. Your bodies won't be found anywhere near here and he'll be out of the country by then."

A sense of utter defeat invaded Laura's mind. Was there anything she could do? There must be a way to warn Hollis. She rose to her feet. Branson jerked in response. "I just want to look out the window," she said.

Branson edged closer to her as she made her way across the plush carpet.

She looked out, pressing her hand on the glass. Far down the mountain, a light appeared and then blipped out of view, swallowed up by the forest. That had to be someone looking for her.

"So much territory to cover. How are you ever going to get Hollis alone?"

"I have a man tracking him. He has some bait he can put out. Your coat and gloves covered in blood."

A lump formed in her throat. This felt so hopeless.

Please, God, at least let Hollis live.

The headlights of a car appeared up the road and then stopped by a house that appeared in silhouette against the night. No lights were on. A lot of these homes were probably only occupied part of the year or, like this cabin, they were vacation rentals. Hollis and the police were out there looking for her, but they were running out of time.

Without turning to look, she knew that Branson had stepped even closer toward her. The threat of violence hung in the air. His proximity was meant to remind her not to try anything.

Then she saw headlights coming toward this cabin. Some distance away but headed in this direction.

Branson erupted. "Kill the lights."

She didn't move.

He pulled his gun. "Now."

There were only two lights on in the living room. Branson clicked off the wall light as he headed toward a door. "Get the one in your bedroom." He retreated to an adjoining room.

She ran to her room, scanning everywhere for something to break a window, or to somehow let the approaching car know that someone was here.

Branson stood in the doorway and aimed his gun at her. "Turn it off."

She complied. Though it was nearly pitchblack, she heard Branson's footfalls. He must have taken a few steps into the living room.

She knew from having looked out the living room window earlier that there were no cars parked outside, no indication that anyone was here. The bottom floor probably had a huge garage to hide cars in. There had to be only one reason someone was approaching. They were looking for her.

A doorbell dinged, the sound reaching all the way up to the third floor. A thud indicated that Branson was leaning his body against the wall just outside the bedroom. She reached out for the dresser that she knew was by the door. Her hand felt for the open doorway. She could barely make out the outline of the furniture in the living room.

The bell dinged again.

She had only one chance to get the searcher's attention. She hurried across the living room, guessing at where the furniture was. Her knees rammed into something hard. Footsteps pounded behind her.

She raced toward the window that looked down on the driveway. She could see the police car, but not whoever had come up to the door. The door wasn't visible from this window.

She pounded on the window. "I'm here! I'm here!"

Branson grabbed her and pulled her back just as two people appeared beneath the extended roof, headed back toward the car. Branson pressed his hand over her mouth and dragged her across the floor.

His mouth was very close to her ear. He whispered between clenched teeth, "How dare you. I ought to break your neck right now."

Outside, she heard a car engine start up. The headlights illuminated the lower half of the window and then swung in the opposite direction.

Her last hope for staying alive was headed back down the mountain.

Hollis swung his flashlight to illuminate the undergrowth of the forest. He and Marisa and the police officer had split up in order to cover more ground. So far four of the homes had been reached with no sign of Laura or the police car. Another search party had visited a fifth home, a three-story cabin, which had been unoccupied.

His light landed by a barren bush. A colorful object that looked out of place caught his attention. He moved in closer and reached for it. A pink glove. He leaned down for a closer look. Laura's glove with bloodstains on it. Hollis's stomach churned. He feared he might throw up.

He called out to the others but didn't get a response. They must have moved too far away. He was about to reach for his phone when he saw a coat lying in a flat area not too far from the glove. His heart pounded as he refused to accept what he was seeing. Laura could not be dead. He hurried over to where the coat was but did not pick it up as he knew that it might be evidence in a crime. He prayed he was wrong. The coat was bloodstained and ripped.

Hollis lifted his head and took in a raspy breath.

He struggled to regain control of his runaway emotions. He was a trained agent and now it was time to use those skills.

Swallowing the lump in his throat, he surveyed the overgrowth, the coat and the glove. And that's when it hit him. Something about this felt really off. Staged. He'd viewed enough crime scenes to know.

He reached for his phone to call Marisa, but a force grabbed him from behind. He dropped his phone as a hard object hit the back of his head. He was still conscious but light-headed and swaying. He turned and swung at the body behind him. His punch was weak.

A fist collided with his solar plexus, knocking the wind out of him. He struggled to breathe and to remain conscious. He was dragged a short distance. His hands were yanked behind him and bound. He was shoved into the back seat of a car. His cheek rubbed against the leather upholstery as the car started to roll.

His head throbbed and he was still wheezing in air. He had to stay conscious. "What has happened to Laura? You know, don't you?"

He stared at the back of the man's head, waiting for the answer that never came. He saw then that the man was dressed in a police uniform.

He tried to lift his head to see out the window. He saw nothing but trees.

The car came to a stop. He heard a mechanical noise, a garage door opening. The car pulled forward. With much effort, he lifted his head again. He was inside a large garage. A police car and a van were also parked inside. The car he was in was some sort of upscale SUV.

The driver got out and as the garage door shut, he took out his phone and made a call.

Hollis struggled to get into a sitting position, but it was difficult with his hands tied.

The thug who had driven him opened the back door. "Get out."

Hollis scooted to the edge of the seat and swung his legs, so they hung out of the car. When he leaned his upper body forward, he could not get enough momentum to rise to his feet. The thug grabbed his arm and pulled him to a standing position.

A man holding a suitcase stood not too far from the SUV. The thug tossed the keys toward him. "The car's all yours, boss."

The man was tall and well-groomed. Though he wore clothes meant to make him look outdoorsy—a flannel shirt and khakis—everything looked pressed and starched. He held a bright yellow down coat. There was something vaguely familiar about him.

The thug pulled Hollis away from the car. The well-dressed man walked over to the SUV, and after stowing his suitcase in the back along with the yellow coat, he opened the driver-side door with a backward glance at Hollis. His expression was one of triumph.

"Have a good flight, sir," said the thug. "I'll let you know when the job is finished."

Hollis knew in that moment that he was staring at the man who had planned all the robberies.

The man got into the car. The thug drew a remote control out of his uniform pocket and pressed the button that opened the garage door. The man backed the car out and turned around. Just as the garage door closed, Hollis saw the red glare of the taillights as the man he'd been hunting for over a year drove away.

The pounding of footsteps on stairs brought his attention back to the open door that led to the rest of the house. His breath caught when Laura emerged, followed by a smirking Branson.

Hollis took a step toward Laura, but the thug grabbed his bound hands and pulled him back. "Stay put."

Laura's eyes searched his.

Branson spoke. "Well, well, well, look who we have here. Mr. Undercover Agent." Branson pushed Laura farther into the garage. Hollis saw then that her hands were bound in front of her. She was wearing a man's coat that was too big for her.

"You better get going," said the thug. "The clock is ticking on this one."

Branson pushed Laura deeper into the garage, then opened the back of the van, directing Laura to get in.

Laura glanced at Hollis. Her gaze held a pleading quality. He had to find a way to escape. His eyes searched the garage. There were tools on the wall that might be useful, but there was no way to get to them.

Branson directed his comment to the thug. "Your share of the loot is sitting on the passenger seat of the van."

"Thanks," said the thug.

"The remainder of your pay will be wired to you once you send photographic evidence that the job is complete," Branson said.

Hollis tensed—he knew that the job Branson was referring to was killing him and Laura.

While Branson got into the police car, the thug directed Hollis toward the back of the van. Hollis crawled in beside Laura. He leaned his shoulder against hers.

"I'm so glad you're still alive," he whispered.

She turned to face toward him. "I had hoped that they wouldn't catch you. Oh, Hollis, I'm so afraid. What are we going to do?"

"I don't know. We have to find a way to escape."

The thug stuck his head in. "Quit jabbering."

The last thing Hollis saw before the van doors slammed shut was the garage door opening and Branson driving away. The police car would provide the perfect cover. Hollis clenched his teeth. The only thing that upset him more than seeing Branson getting away was knowing that the mastermind had also evaded capture.

The thug got behind the wheel and backed the van out. He left it running while he must have been returning the remote.

In the brief seconds while the thug was gone, Hollis took in his surroundings. The back of the van had no windows. No way to see out or get someone's attention. Marisa and the other officer would find the glove and coat, but what conclusion would they draw? The drive from where he had been abducted to the house was hazy, but it had probably taken less than ten minutes.

The thug returned. He glanced over his shoulder at them and then turned to look out the windshield. Hollis found that if he leaned forward and lifted his head he could see through the windshield. The house they were backing away from was a three-story cabin, probably the one that had already been contacted. It was unlikely that Marisa would come in this direction, since this cabin had been deemed to be unoccupied.

The thug turned the van around and headed down the road, driving Laura and Hollis toward inevitable death.

TWENTY

Though she'd been given a man's coat to wear, she shivered as she sat close to Hollis. From fear as well as cold.

The van jerked, indicating that the road they were on was rough. She wondered if the man driving them, the man who had pretended to be a police officer, had turned off the main road. Arthur's plan had been that their bodies be found miles from the cabin. Maybe the thug was going some place so remote that they would never be found.

Hollis leaned close to her ear and whispered, "Pocketknife in coat." He then lifted the hip that was closest to her.

She glanced at the driver, who kept his attention on the bumpy road.

It took some effort to angle her body and maneuver her bound hands to dig into Hollis's coat pocket.

"He's looking." Hollis's whispered warning

made her put her hands back in front of her and sit down. She glanced at the thug, who watched her with a probing gaze before turning his attention back to driving.

When the van was not shaking and rattling as much, she figured they must be on a smoother road. Once she was sure the driver wasn't going to glance in the back, she tried again to get the pocketknife. This time she succeeded.

She stared down at it, grateful that it had a push-button release. She clicked it open, cringing at the sound that it made, but the thug had not heard it over the rumble of the car engine. Hollis turned sideways to her and lifted his arms away from his back. Holding the knife with bound palms together and sawing the rope without cutting Hollis proved to be a challenge. Every time the thug cleared his throat or shifted his weight, they returned to their sitting positions.

Gradually she got through several layers of rope. Hollis wiggled his hands and freed himself. "Put the knife back in my pocket. I'll cut you loose after I take care of him."

She opened her mouth to protest. Wouldn't it be better if they were both free and could take him on?

The van had been slowing down for a few seconds and now came to a full stop.

Hollis leaped to his feet as the rope fell on the floor. The thug had half turned his head when Hollis landed a blow to his cheek and then a fist to his windpipe.

The action only seemed to anger the man as he grabbed Hollis and slammed his head against the console.

Laura walked on her knees to the back of the van. The banging and the grunting told her that the men were in an intense wrestling match. She reached for the handle that would open the back doors. In order to get any leverage on the handle, she had to curve her torso around. The door catch clicked, and she pushed one of the doors open with her elbow. The blackness of night and winter chill greeted her.

The van shook from the intensity of the two men fighting. She turned back around to see that the thug loomed above Hollis, who was lying on his back, partway on the passenger seat. She moved to try to help him any way she could. As the thug lifted his fist to hit Hollis in the face, she heard a click and then the thug howled in pain and gripped his upper arm. He backed away from Hollis and then bent forward as he slumped into the driver's seat. She was close enough to watch as Hollis put the pocket-knife away at the same time he pulled his legs up and swung them around. Hollis pushed open the passenger-side door and jumped out.

The thug, still gripping his bleeding arm, moved his attention to Laura.

She backed away as he slipped between the seat to the cargo area of the van. He lunged toward her. She fell on her behind but kept scooting toward the open doors. The thug touched her foot just as Hollis reached in and grabbed her under her arms, pulling her free.

Hollis lifted her to her feet. The thug was at the open doors preparing to jump out and come after them.

"Run," Hollis yelled.

She spun around and took off. Her bound hands made running awkward. When she glanced over her shoulder, Hollis was punching the thug.

She jogged downhill, not seeing any artificial light. They must have been driven deep into the forest. She found her way to the road they'd probably taken to get here.

Hollis caught up with her. "He's getting back in the van to come after us." He pulled on her sleeve, diverting her away from the road. They moved past some rock outcroppings into a forest that had either been thinned, or affected by fire. The evergreens had few branches and a thick layer of deadfall covered the ground.

She could hear the van's engine humming. When she glanced sideways, the headlights became visible in her peripheral vision. The thug had left the road and was headed toward them. She prayed that the deadfall would be too cumbersome to get over.

Hollis slowed his pace to stay close to her.

The headlights found them. Engine noise pressed on her ears as she willed herself to run faster.

Hollis wrapped his arms around her waist and pulled her off to the side just as the van surged forward. They fell on the ground. His body and the thickness of the deadfall cushioned the impact.

Off to the side, she could hear the motor of the van grinding and the shifter screeching. The thug had gotten the van stuck. He was trying to rock it free by going in reverse and then jolting forward. The abrasive noise indicated he wasn't having much success.

She rolled off Hollis but could not get to her feet without his help.

She held her hands toward him. "Quick. Cut me loose."

Hollis pulled out his pocketknife and bent toward her wrists to see better. He sawed quickly and efficiently, freeing her hands just as they heard a car door slam. The thug was coming after them on foot.

They took off into the night.

Here there was less deadfall to hinder them, and they ran as fast as they dared in the darkness. Several times, Hollis stumbled when he didn't see a log or root.

He glanced over his shoulder. The thug had a flashlight and was closing in fast.

A single shot was fired in their direction. They both ran faster. Because the trees were so sparse there was no place to take cover.

Again, Hollis looked behind him. He could see the glow of the thug's phone as he held it close to his face. He must have figured he couldn't catch them and was calling for help. Was Branson still around? Or maybe some of the guys from the jewelry-store robbery had been ordered to remain close.

Once they were safe, Hollis's number-one priority would be to stop the mastermind of the robberies from getting away. There were two airports he could have gone to. An international one that was fifty miles away, in Bozeman, and a small regional one that was just outside of the resort. Many of the people who lived here flew in for vacations on private and small chartered planes. He assumed that's where the master-mind was headed.

First, he and Laura needed to get out of danger and find a way to contact Marisa and the other law enforcement. He had lost his phone when the thug had caught him. They ran on through the dark not seeing any sign of other homes. When they were at a high spot, where they had a view down the mountain, he still saw nothing.

How far had they been driven? The ride must have been less than twenty minutes, but they were obviously far from civilization.

As they walked, the snow grew deeper, with drifts everywhere. One of Hollis's boots sunk down to the knee.

After pulling his foot free, he stopped to study the landscape, choosing a direction where it looked like the snow wasn't as deep.

Laura stopped to button up the oversized coat she'd been given. The night chill was starting to sink into his skin as well. More than anything, he fought to not give in to defeat. If they stayed out here through the night, they could die from exposure and the knowledge of what the mastermind looked like and where he was going would die with them.

Laura, who did not have gloves, had been walking with her hands in her pockets. She pressed closer to him as they slowed their pace. The one thing he knew was that they had to keep moving.

"It seems like we should at least see some lights somewhere," she said.

"I think he took us to the most remote place he could," Hollis said.

Though they were mostly moving downhill, their path was based on walking where they wouldn't sink into the snow. The stillness of the night surrounded them as snow twirled out of the sky.

The trees grew denser and less barren. This part of the forest must not have been affected by the fire. None of the trees were blackened by fire.

A sort of rumbling bass noise that seemed out of place permeated the forest. Hollis stood still and reached a hand out to stop Laura. "Do you hear that?"

She shook her head.

This time he heard nothing. He waited. He was about to take a step when he heard it again. "I think that's a man shouting." He turned to where he thought the noise was coming from, but saw nothing, so they kept going.

After a few minutes, he stopped, waiting for the sound again. This time, it was more distinct—definitely a human voice. Both of them moved a little faster as they worked their way through a snowdrift.

As they approached, the voice became crystal clear. A man shouting. "I am telling you I can't find you. GPS is leading me in circles."

Through the trees, Hollis had a view of the man as he stood by his car with his back to them. Soldier. He must have been sent to find the thug and then hunt down Hollis and Laura.

Soldier held the phone and listened while the other man must have been talking. Then he said, "Look, I'm going to head up this road slowly. You need to get on it and start walking. I don't care if it's warmer in the van. I can't find you otherwise." Soldier clicked the phone off.

When he turned sideways, both Hollis and Laura stepped back deeper into the forest. Hollis looked at Laura and nodded. This was their only chance to take on Soldier before he drove away.

They had only seconds to strategize. "I'll take him head-on," Hollis told her. "You circle around from the back."

Laura split off and Hollis stepped into the open. Soldier was reaching for the handle of the car door when he looked up and saw Hollis. Soldier reached inside his coat and pulled out his gun. With his attention on Hollis, he didn't hear Laura until she leaped on his back. Soldier swung around in an effort to shake off Laura, but she held on.

The moment of inattention was enough time for Hollis to grab for the gun. Laura pulled Soldier's hair, causing him to yelp. Hollis wrestled away the gun and pointed it at Soldier, who managed to throw off Laura. She landed on her behind in the snow.

Hollis aimed the gun at him. "Your phone. Give Laura your phone. Keep one hand in the air where I can see it."

Soldier grinned. "Got to hand it to you, Mr. FBI. You are tenacious."

The gun was steady in Hollis's hands. "Laura, take that scarf from around his neck and use it to tie his hands behind his back."

Laura got Soldier tied and they put him in the back of the car. When he peered in the car, he saw that the keys were still in the ignition. "You'll need to drive. I'll keep a gun on Soldier and call Marisa."

Laura swung open the driver-side door and sat behind the wheel. She had started the car even before Hollis could get into the other seat.

He buckled his seat belt and then looked back at Soldier. "Don't try anything."

Soldier shook his head. "If there's not a payout for me, I don't do a thing."

Hollis kept one eye on Soldier while he

punched in Marisa's number on the phone. "I have no idea how far away we are from the airport outside of the resort."

"Maybe Marisa can get there before we can." Laura sped up. The car continued down the road as the snowfall intensified.

"Maybe. All the same, we better hurry. I don't want that man getting away."

TWENTY-ONE

Laura pressed the gas, going as fast as she dared as conditions worsened. Snow slashed across the windshield and the wipers worked furiously to clear the glass.

Hollis reached Marisa and explained the situation to her. He added, "You'll have to send a search party up to rescue the man who was chasing us. His van is stuck and he's walking. As soon as I get an idea of where we're at, I'll text you the location."

Soldier spoke up from the back seat. "We're on Moose Peak, I doubt GPS will work up here. It didn't for me."

Hollis relayed the information.

That Hollis showed concern for the man who had tried to kill them was a testament to his character.

Hollis stared at the phone after he said goodbye to Marisa. He spoke to Soldier. "That man's number is in here, I assume."

"Yeah, it's under Bob," said Soldier.

"You need to tell him to go back to the van and wait. He won't believe me." While Hollis found the number, he unbuckled his seat belt and turned to Soldier.

Laura gripped the wheel tighter. "Hollis, be careful. The road is getting slicker by the second."

"I know but I don't want anyone to freeze to death." Hollis leaned over the seat so Soldier could speak into the phone.

Once he disconnected, he turned back around and buckled up.

Laura rounded a curve. She had enough visibility to see lights off in the distance, dotting the landscape. The sight almost made her cry.

Up ahead, she could just make out a crossroads. "Which way?"

Hollis looked at a map on the phone. "Left. Marisa is going to meet us at the airport outside of the resort. She's also alerted locals at the international airport outside Bozeman to be on the lookout for the man we saw back at the cabin."

"He goes by the name Arthur Richards. That's not his real name but that might be the name he's flying under."

"That might be helpful, Laura, thanks." Hollis got back on the phone and relayed that information to Marisa.

Laura made the left turn. Up ahead, she saw a cluster of lights that had to be Lovell Heights by the resort.

"You should see the road that leads to the airport before you get to Lovell Heights."

Lights and road signs became murky from all the snowfall. As she drew closer to the city, she watched for the exit to the airport. She could see the control-tower lights after she made the turn. The conditions were getting even icier as they approached the small airport. Hollis had been texting while she drove.

"Marisa is waiting for us just inside Departures. She'll send a police officer out to deal with Soldier so we can focus on the search."

As Laura pulled up to the curb, a uniformed officer emerged and walked toward their car. Once the officer had Soldier in custody, she and Hollis hurried inside.

Marisa and another officer were waiting just inside the sliding glass doors. Laura glanced around. The airport, which only had two gates, was full of waiting passengers. It wasn't until she saw some of the passengers carrying wrapped packages that she realized it was two days before Christmas.

Marisa approached them. "There have been some flight delays because of the storm. We've done a search of the passengers. No one matching the description you gave me. It would take a warrant to get the names of the passengers from the airlines."

Laura looked up at the board, where she saw that the three pending flights had all been delayed. "Will they even take off tonight?"

Marisa shifted her weight. "I asked the ticket agent. He seems to think the flight headed south will still be a go."

"We need to search this whole airport," Hollis said. "The restrooms as well as all the hallways. Anywhere someone might hide."

They had no idea which flight the man might be on, or if he was even here. "What if he's on one of the flights that likely won't take off tonight? He'll just go back to his car and drive to the international airport in Bozeman."

"Laura's right," Hollis said. "We'll search the parking lot and see if we can find the SUV he was driving. You and the officer can keep searching the airport."

It was possible that Arthur had made arrangements for the car to be picked up by Branson or someone else. Or perhaps it had been a rental. Regardless, this was their last chance, so they had to cover all the bases.

Laura and Hollis stepped back out into the storm. Time was running out.

The snow slashed against Hollis's exposed skin like a thousand cold needles. Their heads down, he and Laura hurried back to the car. Hollis got behind the wheel and turned the heat on full blast. He drove slowly through the parking lot, up and down the rows.

Laura shook her head. "I don't see Arthur's SUV anywhere."

The darkness and the storm had reduced visibility. It was too cold to get out and walk through the lot. "Let's search the lot one more time." With the snow piling up on the cars, it would be even harder to find the one they were looking for.

Once again, he eased by the first row of cars. Laura pressed her face close to the window. When she turned her head, she sat up straighter.

"What is it?"

She pointed toward the edge of the parking lot. "That police car. I can't see for sure, but I think a man in a yellow coat just got into the passenger side."

Hollis sped up. There had been two police cars parked outside of Departures when they arrived. Now there was only one. But one of them could have taken Soldier to jail, or it could be the car they were headed toward. Hollis sped toward the edge of the airport parking lot. The snow was coming down even faster. The police car got on the road that led away from the resort. That meant it was not the police car with Soldier and the real officer taking him into Lovell Heights.

"Call Marisa. Tell her where we're headed and why. We'll need some backup."

While Laura made the phone call, Hollis concentrated on driving in the hazardous conditions.

Laura clicked off the phone. "Marisa and the officer are headed this way."

Hollis followed the patrol car, hanging back but keeping the taillights in his view. He was grateful the low visibility created by the storm made it so that neither Branson nor the man called Arthur Richards could recognize the vehicle Soldier had driven. At this point, they still had the element of surprise on their side.

Hollis surged forward only to have his car fishtail and swerve across the yellow line. He let up on the gas and regained control, reminding himself that all they could do was stay close and wait for Marisa.

The wipers whooshed across the windshield. Laura gripped her armrest and stared straight ahead.

A set of headlights appeared in the rearview mirror. Not the police car, but a dark-colored truck. The truck pulled into the left lane, preparing to pass. It gained speed and then kept going faster, making it clear it intended to pass the police car as well.

The truck surged ahead of the police car but then spun in the middle of the road. Branson must have slammed the brakes, which caused the police car to go out of control. The truck stopped but took up both lanes. The police car crashed into the driver's side of the truck with such force it moved the truck sideways several feet.

Hollis pumped his brakes to keep from crashing into the other two vehicles.

Before he came to a stop, a man dressed in dark clothes exited the passenger side of the police car and ran into the surrounding trees.

Before he could tell Laura to remain in the vehicle, she got out at the same time he did. Down the road, he saw the headlights of an approaching police car. Marisa and the officer, he hoped. Branson had not gotten out of the crashed car yet. Fully aware that they might be walking into a trap, Hollis approached the crash.

The driver of the truck had scooted across the seat and gotten out on the passenger side. The young man was walking and didn't appear to be hurt, though his wide-eyed expression suggested he was in shock.

Hollis gestured that Laura needed to hang back. The whole front end of the police car was crumpled from the crash. Because of the angle of impact, the driver's side had taken the brunt of it. The airbags had not deployed for whatever reason. Branson was slumped over the steering wheel, probably unconscious.

The other police car was getting closer, but Hollis couldn't wait. "Call an ambulance. Tell Marisa where I went and to follow me," he told Laura. The officer with Marisa could remain behind to ensure that Laura wouldn't be in danger if Branson came to.

He set off to chase Arthur into the woods unarmed. He didn't want to risk that Arthur would make another phone call and simply get someone else to come pick him up.

The path of the footprints was easy enough to follow in the fresh fallen snow.

Arthur appeared to be in good shape and moving fast. Hollis didn't see him anywhere, not even when the trees opened up to a flat area. Only the footprints told Hollis which way to go. Hollis entered another wooded area. He had to assume that Arthur was armed, but so far he wasn't even sure he could catch up with the man.

The forest canopy was thicker, making the footprints less obvious without as much snow. Hollis slowed down. He was out of breath. He heard a voice and moved toward it, stepping carefully to keep from making noise. He spotted Arthur.

As he spoke on the phone, Arthur's back was to him. "Yes, it looks like there's a road that leads to someone's house." Arthur looked out through the trees, where he must have noticed a road. "You can track me with your phone. I have to keep moving in case overzealous lawmen get any ideas."

This was Hollis's only chance. He sprinted across the five yards that separated the two men. Arthur whirled around, reaching inside his coat and pulling out a gun just as Hollis crashed into him and knocked him to the ground.

"You." Rage filled Arthur's voice.

Hollis braced the arm that held the gun with his knee before the other man could lift his hand to fire. The other knee pressed into Arthur's chest. "Drop the gun." Hollis clamped his hand on Arthur's throat, making it almost impossible for the other man to move.

Arthur complied and let go of the gun. Hollis knew if he tried to get the weapon, it would mean letting pressure off Arthur's neck and chest, making it easier for him to attack.

He reached for the gun. Though his shooting arm was still pinned, Arthur rolled his body and punched Hollis hard in the back several times.

In pain, Hollis got to his feet, stumbling backward. He steadied his hand and held the gun on the man he had been chasing for so long. "Get up and start walking, arms in the air."

Arthur sneered but did as he was told.

Hollis fell in behind him. They walked through the trees into the open area. Marisa met him when he was almost back to the road. Together they led Arthur to the police car. Two ambulances had arrived and were transporting Branson and the driver of the truck.

Once Arthur was in the police car, Laura got out of the car, where she'd been waiting.

She walked toward Hollis. "So it's over. He's in custody."

"Yes, you can go back to your old life now. I'm sure George the aloe-vera plant missed you."

He couldn't quite read the expression on her face. Was she sad? Confused? "That is what you wanted, isn't it?" He stepped closer to her.

"I thought it was at first." She tilted her head. "But now I don't know anymore if it means not seeing you again."

He pulled off his glove and reached out to brush her cheek with his knuckles. Her features softened and he knew what he saw in her eyes—trust and love. She wanted to stay in his life. Was he ready for that? Such a big step. He needed time to think and pray. He took her into his arms. "Tell you what—it's two days until Christmas, why don't you come and spend the holiday with me and my aunt's family?"

"I'd love that, Hollis." She pulled back so she could meet his gaze. There was a question there in her eyes. *Do you love me?*

He wasn't sure how he would answer that.

TWENTY-TWO

The powerful words of the Christmas carol Hollis's family was singing followed Laura as she stepped out on the covered porch to catch her breath and enjoy the beauty of the snow falling. She'd grabbed a throw on her way out.

Celebrating Christmas with Hollis's family had felt like something out of a dream. Christmas Eve service, games, big meals and yummy treats, lots of laughter. Everything she had wanted and prayed for as a lonely little girl. And she had a standing invitation from Hollis's aunt to come back next year.

God did answer prayers, she realized, but on His timeline.

There was only one thing missing. She knew now that she loved Hollis, but did he feel the same way about her?

She looked up to see the soft swirling snow and the glittering stars.

The singing grew louder as Hollis opened

the door, and then it became muffled when he closed it.

He held up his phone. "I just got a call from my supervisor. They've identified who Arthur Brooks really is, he's going to name names. It's just a matter of time before all those involved in the robbery are brought in."

"That's good news." A note of disappointment entered her voice. While she was happy about the investigation ending well, she had hoped that Hollis had followed her out here to talk about their future together...if there was even going to be one. When they were on the snow-covered road, she had thought she had made it clear that she wanted to see more of him. His response had been so reserved and hard to read. Yet, he had invited her here. "I suppose you will be going back to work soon on another case?"

"Yes, I will. I have a little downtime since this investigation was so intense. How about you? Will you go back to your job?"

"Not sure. All of this has been life altering for me." She stared at the ground. Maybe she had mistaken Hollis's sense of decency for attraction. Maybe he didn't share her feelings.

He leaned closer to her. "Is everything okay?"

"It's more than okay. Thank you so much for inviting me to be with your family," she said.

"It has been one of the most wonderful experiences of my life."

Still, she saw such warmth in his eyes. "They like you a lot, Laura."

Laura peered at the family through the window. They had stopped singing and now were settling down to watch a Christmas movie. As Aunt Gin carried a giant bowl of popcorn into the living room from the kitchen, she gestured for Laura to come inside. "Looks like they'll be starting the movie soon." She stared at Hollis.

"I suppose we should go back inside." He glanced out across the property and then stared at the porch floor.

"Yes, I suppose so." Neither of them moved. "Is everything okay with you?"

Hollis licked his lips and shifted his weight from foot to foot. Though he was dressed in a thick sweater, he was obviously starting to feel the chill, as she was. She pulled the throw tighter around her.

"Laura, I'm not totally prepared for this. Once the stores open tomorrow, I promise we'll pick out a real one together."

"What are you talking about?"

He pulled something out of his jeans pocket. "My uncle helped me make this from some scrap metal he had." He opened his palm to reveal a simple ring.

Her breath caught and the chill she felt disappeared. "Oh, Hollis, are you asking me to marry you?"

"Yes, Laura, marry me."

"And your family agrees?"

"They're crazy about you." Hollis took her hand and slipped the ring on her finger.

It was the most beautiful piece of jewelry she'd ever worn.

He kissed her.

When they looked back into the window, the whole family had gotten up from the couch to applaud.

The warmth of their love and support made her heart soar. "Best Christmas present ever." She turned her attention back to Hollis. "I love you."

"I love you, too." Hollis took his bride-to-be into his arms and kissed her again.

* * * * *

If you enjoyed this book,
please look for these other stories
from Sharon Dunn:

Undercover Mountain Pursuit
Crime Scene Cover-Up

Dear Reader,

Thank you for going on the romantic, often dangerous, roller-coaster ride with Hollis and Laura. As I was writing this book, I thought about the importance of prayer and God's timing. Laura closes her heart off to God as a child because He didn't answer her heartfelt prayer and yet that prayer is answered in abundance by the end of the book, when Laura is an adult. That is a long time to wait for God to come through. While I totally understand a child's faith being shaken when answers to prayer don't materialize, I think as adults, we need to learn to trust that God has heard us even if things seem dark and we feel like God has lost our phone number. I loved writing a book that takes place at Christmas, not just because it's my favorite holiday, but because this time of year, I think people's hearts are softer and more open to the gospel just like it was for Laura.

Take care and Merry Christmas!
Sharon Dunn

Get 4 FREE REWARDS!

We'll send you 2 FREE Books plus <u>2 FREE Mystery Gifts</u>.

FREE
Value Over
$20

Both the **Harlequin® Special Edition** and **Harlequin® Heartwarming™** series feature compelling novels filled with stories of love and strength where the bonds of friendship, family and community unite.

HARLEQUIN
PLUS

Announcing a **BRAND-NEW** multimedia subscription service for romance fans like you!

Read, Watch and Play.

Experience the easiest way to get the romance content you crave.

Start your **FREE 7 DAY TRIAL** at www.harlequinplus.com/freetrial.

COUNTRY LEGACY COLLECTION

19 FREE BOOKS IN ALL!

Cowboys, adventure and romance await you in this new collection! Enjoy superb reading all year long with books by bestselling authors like Diana Palmer, Sasha Summers and Marie Ferrarella!

50BOOKCL22